Who Killed Tiffany Jones?

Who Killed Tiffany Jones? is essentially a puzzle. But, unlike a conventional puzzle, in which we are given the correct number of pieces and can expect that each piece will fit neatly into the final solution, in this mystery the reader is sometimes presented with more than one piece that seemingly fits into the same slot. Which is to say that a reader who correctly assesses all the clues and information included in the tale and applies the strictest logic still might not be able to eliminate all erroneous notions about why the victims were killed and who done it.

Part of the fun of constructing and of solving puzzles is that they not be too easy. And *Who Killed Tiffany Jones?* is filled with enough red herrings and blind alleys to assure that the task is complicated enough to challenge even the most scrupulous Jessica Fletcher or Sherlock Holmes wanna-bes. And, again unlike most murder mysteries, since in this tale many of the clues emerge as much from character and dialogue as from circumstances, the difficulty or *fun* is further heightened. The story has been constructed as both entertainment and a puzzle; it requires imagination as well as logic to solve. It is constructed loosely enough so that there are several scenarios that might fit the facts that are presented in the story. Only one, however, in the authors' assessment most reasonably corresponds to every nuance of character and event suggested in the story.

Finally, *Who Killed Tiffany Jones?* is intended as an amusing romp that will challenge the ambitious amateur sleuth. We also hope you thoroughly enjoy the trip and the colorful characters encountered on the way.

(For complete contest rules and details, including eligibility requirements and entry limitations, see page 191.)

Who Killed
Tiffany Jones?

A Novel

"Mavis Kaye"
Created by Bill Adler and Mel Watkins

 Amistad

An *Imprint* of HarperCollins*Publishers*

This novel is a work of fiction. Any references to real people, events, establishments, organizations, or locales are intended only to give the fiction a sense of reality and authenticity, and are used fictitiously. All other names, characters, and places, and all dialogue and incidents portrayed in this book are the product of the author's imagination.

HarperCollins books may be purchased for educational, business, or sales promotional use. For information, please write: Special Markets Department, HarperCollins Publishers Inc., 10 East 53rd Street, New York, NY 10022.

FIRST EDITION

DESIGNED BY SARAH MAYA GUBKIN

Printed on acid-free paper

Library of Congress Cataloging-in-Publication Data

Kaye, Mavis.
    Who killed Tiffany Jones? : a novel / by Mavis Kaye ; created by Bill Adler & Mel Watkins.—1st ed.
        p.   cm.
    ISBN 0-06-621333-9
        1. African American women singers—Fiction.   I. Adler, Bill, 1929–   II. Watkins, Mel.   III. Title.

PS3611.A89 W47 2002
813'.6—dc21

2002066629

02 03 04 05 06 WB/RRD 10 9 8 7 6 5 4 3 2 1

Who Killed
Tiffany Jones?

ONE

Tiffany Jones was the headliner. Her name dwarfed those of the other performers on the Apollo Theater marquee—a lineup that included Boyz II Men, Juvenile, the British band Soul II Soul, and the up-and-coming young comedian Reggie Stone.

And when Kim Carlyle slithered out of her limo in a skin-tight Donna Karan black sheath, she couldn't help feeling a surge of pride as she glanced at the marquee. Tiffany hadn't appeared as the headline act at the Apollo since the early eighties, when she was the reigning queen of disco and Kim was barely a teenager. But in less than a year, Kim had engineered one of the greatest comebacks in recent show-biz history. As her manager and agent, Kim had guided Tiffany back to the top as pop music's hottest star and one of its most glamorous divas.

On this night, Kim didn't concede much in the glamour department. The form-fitting dress accentuated her athletic, perfectly toned body, and a single strand of pearls set off her smooth caramel skin. Taking the arm of her escort and on-again-off-again lover Rick Dupre, a model and well-known soap actor, she glided toward the lobby through a sea of popping flashbulbs. Rick's molded mannequin smile flashed confidently beneath a glistening, chocolate bald pate, and Kim stalked into the theater with the haughty assurance of Naomi Campbell on a fashion catwalk. She seemed more at ease with the attention than her narcissistic escort.

In a sense, she had been thrust into the limelight. A high-school friend had enticed her to take time from her hard-earned position as a twice-decorated New York City detective to check out a *Playboy* magazine shoot on women in law enforcement. She was intrigued but immediately insisted that nudity was not an option. Still, a persuasive photographer had convinced her that there would be no repercussions if she posed in a tight skirt and a loose-fitting patrolman's jersey. The final photo was, by any standard, modest. But Kim's statuesque physique and the oversize uniform top with three buttons opened to reveal just a hint of cleavage was apparently too much for the NYPD brass. She was suspended the day after the magazine hit the stands.

The media hopped on the story and, of course, the magazine fueled the fire, publicizing the furor and inviting Kim to the L.A. mansion where she hobnobbed with celebs from L.A. and New York. It also provided legal council, and during the two years of litigation that followed she became the darling of the entertainment jet set. After being reinstated and receiving a settlement worth more than a million dollars, she quit the force. She was ambitious and wanted to move on. The contacts she had made during that time and her earlier two-year flirtation with pre-law at NYU made entertainment management a perfect career choice. She had quickly picked up a few promising young clients as well as some seasoned performers, like Tiffany, whose careers were in desperate need of rejuvenation. And, as Tiffany's resurgence demonstrated, Kim was very good at what she did.

She had hosted a small, catered party for Tiffany at her Upper West Side apartment earlier in the evening for about twenty guests and well-wishers. Most were friends, but a few reporters and two or three people Kim had never seen before had shown up. When Tiffany and the other guests left for the theater, Kim stayed behind to deal with the caterers and servers. She and Rick arrived late for the show, and by the time they moved past the lobby's huge mural with its galaxy of black entertainment legends, slipped up the stairs, and found their reserved seats in a box overlooking the stage, Reggie Stone, the MC and comic, was finishing his act and preparing to introduce the headliner.

". . . Yeah, somethin's definitely wrong. Why is it that a dog is a man's best friend—by the way, I see that a few of you fellows brought your best buddies to the show tonight—and diamonds are a girl's best friend! Shit! Women got it goin' on, they always out-thinkin' us. If you don't believe me, go down to the pawn shop and see how much they give you for that raggedy-ass mutt when he gets tired and old."

Stone paused, as the crowd chuckled politely.

"Anyway, it's that time—*Apollo show time!* Are you ready?"

After the audience roared its approval, he continued.

"Straight from a record-setting European tour and blockbuster appearance on the *Oprah* show, here she is—the delightful, divine, delicious, and most incomparable, Miss Tiffany Jones. *Apollo,* can I get a witness! Everybody! Stand up. . . . Say, '*Yeah!*'"

As the audience stood and the velvet curtains parted to reveal a tuxedo-clad, sixteen-piece orchestra, the hoots and thunderous applause nearly drowned out the raucous, upbeat version of "Satin Doll," Tiffany's theme song. Stone turned toward the stage entrance in anticipation but, after a thirty-second pause, turned back to the audience.

"Y'all better give it up," he laughed, "you know how sensitive these superstars are. Lemme hear it one more time!"

The crowd roared and the applause escalated. Stone stared at the stage entrance with mock indignation for a minute or so before a stage-hand rushed out and whispered to him. Obviously upset, they both hurried offstage. The band continued playing for a few more minutes before they suddenly stopped; as the curtains closed, the leader and a few others could be seen rushing backstage. Perplexed, the audience quieted momentarily, then began chanting, *"TIFFANY, TIFFANY, TIFFANY . . ."*

Kim knew immediately that something was seriously wrong, and, as the restless crowd continued chanting, she pushed her way out of the box and headed toward the backstage entrance. She was a familiar face among the musicians and stagehands and had no trouble getting to Tiffany's dressing room. The opened door was surrounded by onlookers, including Maria Casells, the singer's hairdresser and personal attendant. Inside, she could hear Stormy, the old gravel-voiced stage manager, a former second-tier comedian and dancer, cursing and screaming for everybody to get out. When he saw Kim, however, he motioned for her to enter.

Tiffany was sprawled on the floor near the vanity, wearing an elegant, sequined stage gown. Her eyes were wide open, and with her mouth agape and heavy beige makeup already caking, her face had taken on the appearance of a grotesque, stony mask. Kim turned away, then out of pure instinct, a throwback to her days on the force, she quickly scrutinized the dressing room.

An overturned chair lay beside Tiffany and a cigarette, which she had apparently been smoking when she fell, lay near her hand. On the floor, a small burn mark could be seen under the ashes. Everything else seemed in order. Nothing on the vanity table appeared to have been disturbed, and the diva's satin Gucci bag and silk scarf hung on a hook next to the table.

"Did anyone touch anything?" she asked Stormy.

"No, I was the first one in here," he said. "Fact, I had to bust down the door. It was locked from the inside. She ain't moved a muscle and ain't nobody touched a thing. I already called the ambulance and the police."

Kim bent over Tiffany and carefully checked her pulse. A tremor went through her body as she gently closed the diva's eyes and, holding back tears, silently stared at her. Before rising, she checked for any marks or abrasions on Tiffany's wrists and neck. There were none. She also noted that Tiffany's jewelry was intact. The gold chain and huge diamond pendant that Tiffany had worn to the party still lay perfectly placed around her neck. The sparkling stone rested on her bosom just above the top of her low-cut gown. Her husband had given it to her before she left on the European tour, and its six-figure price tag had been well-publicized in the press. Flashing back to her old sleuth ways, Kim drew the obvious conclusion—robbery was not a factor. Moreover, there were no signs of a struggle, no apparent wounds. Nothing appeared suspicious. The diva was simply dead.

The police and medics arrived within fifteen minutes. As a precaution, Kim had convinced the theater manager to try to make sure that no one left the theater before the authorities arrived. As far as Kim knew, nobody had. Once Tiffany was officially pronounced dead, homicide detectives were called. They questioned Stormy, Maria, and everyone else who had access to the backstage area. When convinced that Tiffany's dressing room door had been locked from the inside, the detectives finally allowed members of the audience to leave. The stagehands and performers were detained for further questioning even though the doctor's initial finding was that Tiffany had died of cardiac arrest.

Lieutenant Maurice Jackson, a detective who had worked with Kim when she was on the force and they both worked out of the sixth precinct in lower Manhattan, was in charge of the investigation. A gruff, paunchy, and somewhat comical looking dark-skinned man in his midforties, Lt. Jackson was known for his no-nonsense approach and meticulous observance of police procedures—traits that had earned him a promotion and his present position at the Twenty-Eighth precinct. And though their relationship had been, at best, strained during her tenure, he seemed genuinely moved by Kim's grief. Lt. Jackson saw no indication of foul play; nevertheless, he promised to go over the scene with a fine-tooth comb. He also told her that, if she wished, she could hang around and observe. Kim took him up on the offer.

Klaus Svrenson arrived at the theater a little before 1 A.M. The flamboyant international financier and businessman had interests in everything from topless bars and collection agencies to Atlantic City casinos and brokerage houses. He had married Tiffany two years ago. After he was contacted at their Easthampton estate, it had taken him two hours by helicopter and limo to get to Manhattan.

When he spoke to Lt. Jackson, Klaus was shaken and ashen. Kim stood nearby listening. No, Tiffany didn't have a drug problem or a history of heart trouble. There were no recent discoveries of serious illness. Tiffany, however, had been a diabetic for years, something she concealed from many of her closest friends. And during their two-year marriage she had gone into shock on at least one occasion.

After Klaus pointed out that Tiffany always carried insulin and a hypodermic needle in her handbag, the detective carefully unzipped the satin purse and looked inside. He then slipped the purse with its contents into a plastic evidence bag and handed it to an assistant. That discovery seemed to clarify the situation for Lt. Jackson. He consoled Klaus and told him that he had no further questions. If something else arose, he would contact him the next day.

It was Kim who asked if there was anyone who might have reason to harm Tiffany. Klaus bristled at the question and, despite having known Kim for more than a year, reacted with surprising anger. No one would harm his wife, he insisted, before standing and storming from the room. Although his response puzzled Kim, she attributed it to Klaus's shock and stress. Kim also pulled Maria aside and asked about Tiffany's behavior when they arrived at the theater. The shaken attendant said that Tiffany had been sweaty and irritable, although she had taken her insulin in the bathroom at Kim's apartment. It was the first time, she said, that Tiffany had ever asked to be left alone in her dressing room before a performance.

After speaking briefly with Lt. Jackson, Kim met Rick in the lobby and returned to the limo.

When the car arrived at West 99th Street and Riverside Drive, they remained inside for a few minutes, engaged in a heated discussion. Finally, Kim stepped outside and leaned in to speak to Rick.

"Have you lost your mind? I can't believe you'd even think about hooking up after what just happened," she snapped.

"I'm sorry, baby—"

"Look, you can come up if you want, but I'm sleeping alone. Nothing's happening. You understand?"

"Hey, no problem," Rick said, climbing out of the car. "I didn't mean to upset you any more than you already are."

"You got that right," she snapped.

"I just thought you might want to have some company, that's all," he mumbled. He followed her into the brownstone, which was tucked between two high-rise apartment buildings, and up the stairs to her duplex condo.

At 2:45 A.M. Klaus Svrenson checked into the Plaza Hotel. After leaving the theater, he had walked around the block then returned to talk to the police and attempt retrieving some of his wife's belongings. He was even more upset when he left empty handed the second time. In his room, he immediately ordered a quart of Glenlivet from room service. After pouring himself a tumbler of the Scotch, he sat down at the desk and began scribbling a list of names on the hotel stationery. He paused once or twice, lost in thought, and nervously paced the floor before returning to his task. A half hour later, he completed the list of twelve names.

PLAZA HOTEL
Renee Rothchild - Paris
Cheeno (Shaywan Anderson) - Los Angeles
Brian Woods - Las Vegas
Kees Van derVall - Amsterdam
K.J. Hunter - Dallas
Ezekiel Kwabena   - Freetown, Sierra Leone
Dave "Tater" Hamlin - Washington
Josephine St. Claire   - New Orleans
"Ruff Daddy" (Edward Shelton) - Atlanta
Frank Napolini   - Warren, Ohio
Clarence Johnson ("Mojo") - New York
"Sally" - cell phone

After another tumbler of Scotch and fifteen more minutes of pacing, Klaus began the more tedious task of calling each of the individuals on the list. It took more time and effort than he had anticipated since the time zones varied radically. Each conversation took less than ten minutes and, though intense, seemed to go smoothly. When he had finished, however, Klaus appeared more shaken than he was when identifying his wife's body. He carefully folded the list and placed it in a rear pocket of his pants, then sprawled on the bed hoping to get a few hours sleep before sunrise. Besides funeral preparations and the inevitable meetings with the press, there were more calls and even more important arrangements that had to be made as quickly as possible

When Kim awoke the next morning, she slipped into a silk nightgown and went to the balcony overlooking the apartment's first-floor living room area. Rick was no longer on the couch where she had insisted he stay when she went to bed. Apparently he had decided that if they weren't sleeping together there was no reason to stick around and had let himself out during the night. Relieved, she showered, went downstairs, and, after starting a pot of coffee, retrieved the morning newspapers that had been shoved through the slot in the outside door of the brownstone.

The *New York Times* had a brief obituary that chronicled Tiffany's sudden rise to fame as the queen of disco, her fall from grace in the late '80s, her divorce from Thomas Brenner, the volatile music mogul to whom she had been married for ten years, her unexpected marriage to financier and import/export tycoon Klaus Svrenson, and her meteoric resurgence as a chanteuse in 1999. The story did not give a cause of death but, along with Klaus, cited Faith and Emerald, Tiffany's two young children from her first marriage, as survivors.

The *Daily News* hadn't covered the story, but the *Post*, under a typically dramatic headline, DEATH AT THE APOLLO, ran both a photo of Tiffany and a story suggesting that the circumstances of her death were "unusual." Kim read the report carefully, noting that the *Post* emphasized how Tiffany's dressing room door had been locked from the inside, and also how it made much of the unavailability of the star's personal attendant Maria Casells, presumably the last person to see her alive. Apparently, after being questioned by the police, Maria had either refused to talk to reporters or, as the story hinted, "disappeared."

Kim had never been one to put much faith in the tabloid's often lurid insinuations, but the story did get her attention. Reclining on the sofa with coffee and toast as she gazed out of her huge picture window at the Hudson River and New Jersey skyline, Kim decided that if only out of curiosity she would call Maria and talk with her again within the next few days. As she relaxed and riffled through the rest of the paper, another photo and headline caught her attention: SOAP STAR NABBED AT MELEE, the headline read, and underneath it was a photo of Rick in handcuffs, head bent in an attempt to conceal his identity, being hustled out of the Paradox, a well-known gay after-hours club. Kim nearly gagged on her coffee before getting over the initial shock and composing herself. A few moments later, she laughed aloud as she reared back onto the embroidered African-print fabric that covered her Maurice Villency sectional.

"Damn," she muttered, staring at the picture. Shaking her head, she rose and started up the stairs. She wasn't sure why Rick had been at the Paradox, but the thought that he might be hitting from both sides of the plate wasn't a complete shock. Still, the possibility that she had been deceived angered her. That's it for his sorry, lying ass, she thought, as she stepped into the shower. Her next thought was, Thank God for condoms.

TWO

AMSTERDAM—SATURDAY, JULY 14

Kees Van derVall strode into De Prins Grand Café and sat at one of the choice tables in an alcove near the middle of the room without waiting for the maître d' to seat him. He leaned back into the plush golden chair and looked impatiently at his watch.

After fifteen minutes, he began to wonder what could possibly be taking Winthrop James so long. Had something else happened? Kees ran a shaking hand through the unruly dark blond curls that were suddenly pasted to his forehead with sweat. He needed to get home quickly. He hadn't been feeling well all morning.

He blew his nose into a silk handkerchief and stared out of the bay window beside him at the greenish-gray waters of the Prinsengracht. Sea gulls and herons darted back and forth along the tree-lined banks of the canal. On the far side of the water, tourists gazed up at the 400-year-old, bell-gabled canal houses lining the tiny cobblestone street. As far as Kees was concerned, this was one of the most spectacular views in Amsterdam.

But the view couldn't hold his attention for long. Kees was rising to make his way out of the restaurant and down to the offices of Textel International Corporation when Winthrop finally strode through the door. The tall, immaculately dressed Englishman stood in the entranceway and surveyed the room. He sauntered over to Kees's table and extended his hand with a wide smile.

"Kees, my friend, how are you?"

Kees smiled stonily up at Winthrop's pale, lightly freckled face before taking his seat again. "Well, what exactly can I help you with, Winthrop?" he asked, leaning back in his chair. "What's the problem now?"

Without answering, Winthrop unfolded the local newspaper and dropped it on top of the empty plate in front of Kees. Then he sat down and awaited Kees's reaction.

Kees paled visibly as he read the headline: TWO POLICE OFFICERS FOUND DEAD. When Winthrop didn't speak after a few moments, Kees whispered, "What does this have to do with me?"

"Well, my friend, the incident appears to have your signature written all over it. Let's just say that there are those who feel you're drawing too much attention to yourself."

"I don't know anything about it."

"All right, for the sake of argument, let's assume you don't. The problem is the same as it has been in the past. It's nothing we haven't discussed before. For whatever reason, and I'll avoid going into that, things are not moving rapidly enough on your end. You seem to be distracted by other interests. I just wanted you to know that these diversions haven't gone unnoticed. If I were you, I'd be more careful."

Kees blanched. "What are you trying to say, Winthrop?" he shouted. "Get to the point! If you're accusing me of something, say so. But be careful. Unless something has changed, you're just a futionary. You should be worried about your end, which from what I know only involves paper pushing and ass kissing. Why don't you try coming down from your ivory tower and take a look at the real world. As I said," he gestured at the newspaper, "this has nothing to do with me."

"Is that so? Well, then the word on the street is entirely wrong and you're being maligned. And perhaps you're right, maybe I've overstepped my bounds." He smiled. "By the way, did you get a call from New York this morning?"

Kees paused. He wasn't aware that Winthrop knew anything about Klaus. Did his connections stretch that far, or was he just fishing? Kees had the distinct feeling that he was being set up. "No," he said, "did you?"

Winthrop leaned back in his chair and sighed.

"Perhaps this wasn't a good idea. I seem to have put you on the defensive. And that, I assure you, is the last thing that I wanted to do, honestly. My intention was to look out for you and myself as well. Look, the business is our primary concern, and we've both been well rewarded by it. It's far too lucrative to let our individual concerns become an obstacle. I'm headed back to Antwerp this afternoon; I have to meet with some African businessmen. But I wanted to make sure that you were all right before I left."

Winthrop smiled arrogantly. Kees had never liked him, and now he felt like smashing his fist into that smug little British face. He restrained himself, however, and stood up. Two could play at this game of chess.

"I understand what you're saying, and I appreciate your concern. I'll take . . . necessary precautions. Good day, Winthrop."

Winthrop James nodded as Kees turned and strode toward the exit. When he disappeared, Winthrop smiled, picked up the newspaper, and ordered a cup of tea.

d to his flat, he immediately opened the cello-
oin that he had left on the coffee table. He ignored
the ___ l its tenth ring, then, annoyed, picked it up.

"Hallo. Who the hell is it?"

"Kees, my friend, you sound like you're pissed off. Well, so am I. I've heard some disturbing news, and I hope you have a very good explanation. I wasn't happy to hear that you're operating your own private business out of our warehouse." The voice gradually rose in intensity. "Now that wouldn't be so disturbing if you had informed us or properly compensated us. What disturbs me most is that you've also been bragging about it. Do you think that because you're a few thousand miles away, in fucking Amsterdam, that you can't be touched!"

When Kees recognized the voice, he nearly dropped the phone. It was Riccardo Napolini calling from the United States.

"Riccardo . . . I, uh, I intended—"

"Shut up, Kees. We've warned you before and I thought we'd come to an understanding—"

"If this has to do with James—"

"James? No, that's not what this is about. I don't care about that fucking bookkeeper. I don't like his prissy little English ass any more than you do. I'm talking about respect and keeping a low profile. Yeah, he called one of my guys. He wanted to discuss the meeting you had earlier today. But that's not the problem. The problem is my warehouse."

"I know, I know," Kees muttered. "I was going to straighten it all out but—what about this thing with Klaus?"

"Don't worry about that. Klaus panicked because he thinks his wife got whacked. We'll take care of that situation. Your problem is with me and the fucking warehouse. I brought you into this deal. I don't want to be forced to explain any fuckups, you understand? The only reason the annex hasn't been raided yet is because your guy Petris informed us of the difficulties you had there the other day. I made some calls to the local authorities and took care of it. For the time being. And get this straight, I only saved your ass because you're supposed to be handling our business out of there also."

"Riccardo, don't worry, I'll take care of this."

Napolini sighed. "Do I sound worried, asshole? Look, here's what you're going to do. First, you move all of your contraband out of the warehouse. Second, you arrange to have all the money you owe us sent immediately. Someone will let you know where to send it tomorrow. And last, you will concentrate on the business we set up for you — fuck everything else. You will do all this within two days. Don't disappoint me, Kees. Are we clear?"

Kees slammed the telephone back into the cradle. But only after he was sure Riccardo had already hung up. He stood, staring out of the floor-to-ceiling windows that ran the length of his apartment, at the brackish waters of the Brouwersgracht. Pacing back and forth in front of the windows, he tried to think of some way of getting the money owed Napolini's outfit.

As the bells of the renowned Westerkerk tolled in the distance, he felt a familiar, dull ache creeping from the nape of his neck up through the back of his skull. He pinched his nostrils and inhaled deeply. Shit, not right now! He rushed back to the coffee table, trying to fight the urge but knowing that only another line of heroin would do it. Shakily, he opened the bag and poured a small mound of white powder onto the mirror on the coffee table, then cut two neat lines with a razor blade. After greedily snorting both lines, he leaned back on the couch and felt the rush warm his body. His headache immediately began subsiding.

Ten minutes later, he stood, pushed the cellophane bag into his briefcase, and hurried out of the door.

The warehouse was a narrow, red-brick building that dated back to the 1780s. Inside, hundreds of shipping crates were stacked along the walls. They contained artifacts and curios from nearly every country in Europe as well as some rare sculptures and paintings by well-known artists. The artifacts and art work awaited shipment to shops and galleries all over the world. But the real business of the warehouse went on behind the showroom.

Kees pushed his way past the two Indonesian women who dealt with the artists and art patrons that flocked to Kühne's Art Gallery daily. He stalked up the winding staircase, past his own office, and then down a concealed back staircase behind the broom closet at the end of the hall. The staircase led to an annex that had been built in the 1940s to house Jews fleeing Nazi persecution; they hid in secret rooms and passageways, sometimes for years, waiting for liberation. The annex was all but undetectable. How could anyone have found out? Who could I have told? Kees wondered.

At the bottom of the stairs, Kees entered the first of three rooms located two and a half floors below ground level. Off to the right, a dozen men in blue aprons sat hunched over large blocks of heroin, carefully cutting them up, then weighing and packaging the smaller bundles. They didn't notice him enter.

Kees went to a second room looking for his assistant, Kantjil Sabo, and found him sitting on a crate full of AK-47s. He was doing an inventory on three crates of Kalashnikov rifles from Eastern Europe. The rest of the new shipment, at least another dozen crates, waited to be inspected.

"Start packing," Kees shouted, although Kantjil was seated less than three feet from him. "We're leaving. Everything has to go. We have to be out of here by the day after tomorrow."

"Why? What happened?" the young man asked.

"Napolini knows about those two police officers *we* killed."

Kantjil didn't miss the fact that Kees said "those two police officers that *we* killed." He hadn't killed anybody. In fact, he had been out of the room when Kees shot the officers in the back as they bent to inspect a suitcase full of heroin in the tiny room behind them.

"You should have paid them off, Mr. Van derVall. We've operated here without a problem for the past two years—"

Kantjil saw the punch coming, but he couldn't duck fast enough. Kees's fist connected squarely with the bridge of his nose. He crumpled off the edge of the box, hitting his head as blood spurted across the cold, tiled floor. Kees pulled a .45 caliber pistol from his waist holster, cocked it, and leveled it at Kantjil's head.

"Don't ever question me again," Kees said. "Do you understand me? Now start packing. All of it. I'll call you and tell you where to take it later."

Kees strode up the stairs and out of the building. But once he was settled in the plush seat of his Lexus, he realized that he didn't know where he wanted to go. He was too upset to go home. So he headed to the only other place that he could think of.

He drove to a tiny cobblestone street called Snoekjessteeg Centrum. To the right, a two-story, salmon-colored townhouse stood directly behind a five-floor apartment building. Kees parked out front and went inside.

The townhouse was actually an exclusive coffee shop. In fact, you couldn't get in if you didn't know someone. The person Kees knew was his old friend Petris. At least he had thought that he knew Petris. Now he wasn't so sure.

Black leather couches lined the walls and club music throbbed in the background. Large-breasted women in bikini tops, halters, and miniskirts waded through the smoky crowd selling top-quality marijuana from colorfully decorated menus. Magic mushrooms and Ecstasy also flowed like water.

But Kees didn't want anything that the beautiful waitresses offered. He'd brought his own. He settled into a seat and lifted the plastic bag from his suitcase.

By midnight, Kees was even more wired. He still didn't want to go home. Unable to think of anything else to do and with nobody else to call, Kees rang up Kantjil and insisted that he go out to a club with him. Unwilling to upset his boss any further, Kantjil grudgingly agreed.

After a few failed attempts to get into the trendy, upscale clubs, they wound up at a small, seedy hip-hop club called Frankie's. There was sawdust on the floor and a stained-glass picture of Satan drinking blood from a crystal goblet on the wall above their heads. The seats were sticky and Kantjil sat gingerly so as not to dirty his clothes. Kees didn't even notice the gummy residue on the back of his slate-gray Hugo Boss suit.

Sometime during the night, Kantjil left. Kees didn't remember when. Nor did he remember where or when he had gotten into a brawl. But when he woke soon after dawn lying facedown on the bank of the Amstel River, he suspected that he had. Unable to find his car, he staggered to his feet and unsteadily began walking toward his home.

As he walked, the events of the previous day played out in his mind. He didn't care about James or the dead policemen; his real concern was that his business was being put in jeopardy. Kees had to admit, even to himself, that he had been damned foolish. But what could he do about that now? How would he pay Riccardo and the Napolini family? He had put some cash away but it wasn't enough to cover what the Napolinis would want.

Kees looked back over his shoulder as he walked. He couldn't shake the feeling that someone was watching him, following him no matter which way he turned. Before the call from Klaus he had felt untouchable, totally in control. But now, even though Riccardo had assured him there was nothing to worry about for at least two days, he felt vulnerable.

When Kees got back to his flat, he found the door ajar. The sight of the open door sobered him instantly and he pulled out the .45 he carried in his holster. He crept silently into the house and looked around. The place had been ransacked. Tables were turned over, pictures slashed, the cushions on the leather sofa ripped open. His mattress had been slit open as well. And the bed had been pushed away from the wall. Kees holstered his gun and frantically shoved the bed out of the way. The safe that he had had built into the wall behind the bed was open. It was empty. His cash was gone.

Head reeling, Kees slumped down onto the couch. No one had that combination. There were no signs that the safe had been forced open. It didn't make sense. He ran to his closet and dug around through the heap of trampled, shredded clothes on the floor. Beneath a concealed panel in the floorboards, he found what he was looking for. Thank God, Kees thought as he removed a thick envelope stuffed with cash and a notebook containing the records of his drug-smuggling operation and names of his private African contacts. He tore out the pages, placed them in an ashtray, and set them on fire. At least they couldn't document his outside revenue and sources.

After two hours of sleep, Kees showered and dressed before going to look for his car. It was nearly three o'clock when he found it.

An hour later, Kees stood in front the large home of his old friend and business partner, Petris Nicholov. It was Petris who had introduced him to Riccardo and the Napolini family. The thought that Petris may have betrayed him was too much for Kees to handle. He pushed down hard on the bell with one hand and banged on the door with the other.

The door swung open. In one fluid motion, Petris reached out, grabbed Kees by the collar, pulled him inside, and shut the door.

"Are you mad?" Petris demanded. "You can't make that kind of commotion in a neighborhood like this. The police will be here before you can get to the other end of the street."

"Someone broke into my flat. Whoever it was wrecked the place and emptied the safe."

Petris's eyes hardened. "So why are you telling me? What are you trying to say?"

"I'm saying that whoever broke in knew the combination."

"And since you obviously have no other friends, your skewed logic convinced you that I had to be in on it somehow," Petris said. "The only problem is that I never knew your combination. Now, unless you're accusing me of mind reading as well, I think you should leave, Kees."

"Don't bullshit me! I know that you told Riccardo Napolini or someone in his crew about the drugs and the policemen."

Petris stepped in so close to Kees that they were almost touching. "So?"

"So? Is that all you can say? I thought we were brothers."

"If you want to force the truth, fine. Let's deal with it. You're a fool, Kees. A damned fool. You leave too many loose ends. You don't think before you act. Yeah, I talked to Riccardo. I wanted to make damned sure he knew I wasn't involved in your shady side operations."

"Yeah, protecting your own ass," Kees said. "But there's one thing you both seem to forget—what I do on my own time is my business. Nobody else's. The Napolinis don't own me. I work with them, not for them."

Petris laughed and shook his head. "Kees, you're a friend of mine. I've known you for years, but I think you've misunderstood something. Perhaps you don't know who you're dealing with. When you entered the deal with the Napolinis, agreed to handle *their* business and use *their* warehouse, you sold part of yourself. When you bring something else into their premises, they expect part of it. I wouldn't try to squirm out of that deal if I were you."

Frustrated and enraged, Kees stared at Petris for a moment, then stormed out the door. Without even thinking, he headed back toward The Den.

It was dark when Kees lurched unsteadily out of The Den. He tried to convince himself that his anxiety resulted from the drugs, but he still couldn't shake the suspicion that someone had been watching him all evening. And after what had happened earlier in the day, he wasn't anxious to go home. As he walked down Oude Hoogstraat, he quickened his pace and glanced over his shoulder several times. Nothing seemed unusual. There didn't appear to be anyone suspicious on the street. But it didn't allay his fears. He was certain someone was watching him, waiting for him to slow down, to drop his guard. Struggling not to panic, he made a quick right turn onto OudeZijds Achterburgwal, into the red-light district. As usual, the area was crowded with men ogling the working girls who sat behind large picture windows lit by red fluorescent lights.

Kees tried to blend into the crowds lingering around the sex shop doorways and the prostitutes' windows, but he still felt conspicuous. Sweating heavily, his anxiety building, he stared blankly into the sex shop near him and tried to compose himself. Someone tapped him on his shoulder, and he turned abruptly, instinctively reaching into his jacket for his gun.

"Hallo, mister. Would you like to come in, ya?" a beautiful young woman asked as she leaned out of the doorway next to him.

Kees sighed with relief.

She was dressed in a white lace teddy and white stiletto heels, and her long blond hair cascaded down below her waist. He stared at her silently for a moment and was about to turn and walk away, but her smile disarmed him. There was no trace of the empty, cold eyes or telltale haggard look that most often came with the territory. She seemed almost genuine, he thought, almost as if she had been waiting there just for him. And, even as he considered it, he had to laugh at himself. I'm thinking like a trick, he said to himself. She smiled again and motioned for him to come inside. He paused only briefly before following her. The young woman locked the door behind them and closed the curtain over the window looking out on the street.

Nellica was her name, or so she said, and when her shift ended at four o'clock she suggested that they go to a nearby after-hours pub for drinks. Although he wasn't up to more drinks, Kees considered it since he was still trying to decide if he should return to his own apartment. She seemed harmless enough. She had told him that she was twenty and had been working as a prostitute for only six months. Her parents didn't know. They thought she was paying her way through school by working as a receptionist.

As he dressed, Kees let it slip that he had had some problems at his flat so he couldn't go back there until he found a way to clear everything up.

"Well, I've never, ever done this before," Nellica said, after a pause, "but you seem like you're really having some serious troubles. If you'd like, after the pub you can come and sleep at my flat for the rest of the night. I'd like that."

A half hour later, they climbed the four long, steep flights of stairs leading to her tiny attic room at the Hotel America.

"I don't have a real flat," Nellica explained. "I move from hotel to hotel every few weeks."

"Why is that?" Kees panted, trying to catch his breath after the long climb.

Nellica gave a nervous shrug. "Boyfriend troubles. This way, he can't find me."

The nearly bare room was furnished only with an open-face wardrobe made out of plywood, a small table crammed with makeup bottles, and an unmade bed. One small window looked out onto the street. Both the toilet and the shower were down the hallway. Satin panties, lace garters, and leather camisoles were flung haphazardly around the room. Chained to one of the bars of the bed's metal frame and half hidden under a black lace teddy was a pair of metal handcuffs. Kees sat down on the bed, pushed aside the teddy, and rattled the cuffs.

"You're a bad girl now, aren't you," he chuckled.

"No, not really," she snapped. Then, feeling guilty for raising her voice, she explained, "They were here before I got here.

"Whoever left them didn't bother to leave the key. It was probably some sort of prank or something. But it really doesn't matter. I don't do stuff like that during off hours anyway. Doesn't appeal to me."

Kees was silent as Nellica undressed and put on an old T-shirt.

She hadn't meant to snap at him, but she felt terrible, as if she had a horrible hangover even though she'd had only one drink during the evening. When Nellica switched off the light and lay down, Kees lay down next to her, fully dressed.

"Are you comfortable? Don't you at least want to take off your jacket or your pants or something?"

"No. I'm fine, thanks."

Nellica started to say something else, but she was so tired she couldn't seem to form the words. She heard Kees's voice, but it seemed distant, as if it were coming from the end of a long, dark tunnel. Gradually the sound diminished, and she fell into a deep sleep.

When Nellica woke up later that morning, her head was throbbing and her face was sticky with sweat. She tried to sit up and focus, but it was all she could do to keep from throwing up. She turned to her side and suddenly drew back when she realized that someone else was in bed with her. He lay on top of the sheet with his back to her, fully dressed except for shoes and a jacket. Then, remembering she had brought someone home with her last night, she relaxed. A moment later she nudged him softly in the back trying to wake him.

"Hey, hey, mister! Time to get up. I've got to go out."

When Kees didn't respond, Nellica reached around him and began turning him over on his back.

It was then that she felt the viscous moisture on her hand. Frightened, she pulled him over on his back, and gasped when she saw that his neck and the front of his shirt were covered with blood. Nellica scrambled from the bed and slowly backed toward the door. In shock, she stared at the lifeless figure. His left arm was stretched above his head, his wrist locked tightly into one end of the handcuffs, the other end of which was still attached to the bed frame. His eyes were open in a dead man's stare.

When Nellica saw the raw, open gash on his neck, she began screaming and pounding her fists against the door. Kees's throat had been slit from ear to ear.

The police inspectors immediately cordoned off the building after the hotel manager took them to Nellica's room. Her screams had brought hotel staff members as well as a crowd of guests to the hallway outside the room. The police had been called immediately.

They meticulously gathered personal information from everyone who was still inside the hotel. No one escaped the lengthy and methodical questioning.

Some of the forensics experts who combed the room complained that there was evidence of too many people having been on the premises. A preliminary sweep of the place uncovered hair and skin samples of at least two dozen individuals. And none of it was fresh. The Hotel America was a high traffic, transient place. It would take much more time and effort to even attempt narrowing the field down to a likely suspect. The inspector, a middle-aged veteran of the department named Philippe Sally, told them to keep trying.

"Every criminal makes a mistake," he insisted. "There is no such thing as a perfect crime."

THREE

Baltimore

Edward "Ruff Daddy" Shelton—dressed casually in a flowing white linen shirt opened to his navel, matching linen trousers, and Bill Blass sandals—shifted his weight anxiously as he stood near the ticket counter at Baltimore/Washington International Airport. The heavy 24-carat gold chain that hung from his neck glistened in the bright sunlight streaming through the floor-to-ceiling window across from the counters. He was a stocky, camel-colored twenty-eight-year-old whose face was set in a cold, fierce expression. Even his smile was intense. Now he waited impatiently for Wardell Bransford, the skinny young gofer who was waiting in line to purchase his tickets to Atlanta. There were four people ahead of Wardell.

"Damn, who woulda thought we'd end up in Baltimore on a damn Saturday," Ruff Daddy said to Morris Humphreys, the tall, athletic-looking thirty-five-year-old who stood beside him. Mo, as he was called, was his personal bodyguard and head of personnel and corporate security for RuffRoad Records. Despite the heat, he was wearing jeans and a multicolored, designer leather bomber jacket. He wore nothing under the jacket, which was left open to reveal his bulging pecs, the sculpted six pack beneath them, and an array of gold and silver chains that would have made Mister T envious.

"We be out of here directly," Mo said, grinning and flexing his muscular upper body.

"I know that's right." Ruff Daddy laughed, then abruptly cut off his laughter. He and his posse had been on the way to Atlanta when the jet he had leased mysteriously developed engine trouble and had to make an emergency landing in Baltimore. "Yo, son, what's the deal with the Asian bitch in sunglasses over by the courtesy phone?" Ruff Daddy mumbled to Mo. "You checking her out? She's makin' me nervous. Look like she tryin' to signal the Hispanic cat over by the baggage check-in. I'm sayin', what's up with that?"

"You buggin' man. You gettin' par-a-noid. They just checking each other out 'cause they both outta pocket down here with these country hicks. They ain't got nothin' but crackers and pure black folk up in here. Ain't no shades in between. Corny businessmen, farmers, and housewives! That's it. I mean, damn! Whoa-a-a! Look at the haircuts and hairdos. These people still got those old-time 1975-Florida-Evans-Good-Times-Fros."

Mo laughed at his own joke, then sang, *"Don't laugh, hos . . . I'm down with the Afros."*

"Man, you ain't no MC. Why you frontin' like you got some skills? Now pay attention. You suppose to keep us from getting involved in crossfire of any kind whatsoever, dawg."

Mo Hump put on his dark glasses so no one could follow his eyes. He glanced back and forth between the slim Asian woman in dark glasses and the Hispanic near the baggage check-in. Except for the icy scowl on the Asian's face, they seemed harmless enough, and neither one appeared to be packin'.

"I don't think they wit each other," he said. "Look like Chico tryin' to make a play to me. And she ain't goin' for it."

"Anyway, keep an eye out. How'd it be to get blind-sided in Baltimore? Ah, hell naw."

"Don't worry. I feel you."

"No doubt."

Ruff Daddy was a millionaire, but more than a few people suspected that he hadn't accumulated all of his fortune in his chosen profession, the record business. Nobody, not even Mo, knew for sure.

"The source of my income is a subject upon which we need not elaborate," Ruff Daddy had once told Mo, and the tone of his voice suggested that the subject was best left alone.

The profession that Ruff Daddy had chosen was rap music. He was rising fast toward the top of the heap as a rapper, MC, vibe-giver, producer, and, now, record-label owner and icon like P-Diddy, aka, Puff Daddy, from whom he had taken his name, and Master P, whom he had met once but didn't like. And, like Russell Simmons, he wanted to jump mainstream and put hip-hop culture dead at the center of the action.

Ruff and Mo were joking and laughing at the Baltimore locals when Ruff's cellphone rang. "Shelton?" the voice on the other end of the line inquired. It was Kim Carlyle, his agent—she was the only one who called him that—checking to see if he was still going to Los Angeles for the bash being thrown by Cheeno, another of her clients.

"Yeah, I'll be there, soon as I finish the business down here," he said.

"Where are you?" Kim asked.

"You won't believe it, but I'm stuck in Baltimore right now."

He explained that he'd been on his way to hook up with Brixton, a hot new British performer that a London contact had turned him on to. As he spoke, he remembered the last time he'd seen Kim, sitting in the backseat of her limo, dressed in a hot designer outfit, sipping cognac, and taking care of business. She was the one who had jump-started his career, helping to move him from an opening act to a head-liner, but he wasn't quite sure if he could trust her completely. First off, she was a little too controlling and assertive for his taste. That's why he had never moved on her. He was absolutely certain about one thing—he had to be in charge, of his business and his woman.

Kim was more than fine enough to get his attention, but he'd passed. And a year ago they had cut a new deal regarding her position as his representative. When he signed for his own record label he assumed responsibility for booking and promoting himself. She agreed to accept a lesser role and percentage as his agent, and he, in turn, agreed to pressure the acts signing with his label to sign with her as their representative. It had worked perfectly so far. She had a fabulous network, and, whenever possible, she tipped him off about rising stars so he could approach them before Master P or P-Diddy got to them.

Even so, he was not entirely sure of her. He wondered if she didn't sometimes sell him out to a higher bidder. Some of her acts were signed to other labels, and he wondered if she had given someone else first crack at them or if they'd come to her already signed, as she said.

No matter what, as an ex-cop Kim Carlyle was useful, Ruff thought as he listened to her telling him how big Cheeno was going to be. "Stop selling. I'll be there."

They talked for a while longer, and he related the details of the trouble he had had with the leased jet and forced landing in Balti-more. "You know anyone in Atlanta that might be useful if we need help with anything?"

"Contact a detective named Freddy Carmichael. I'll give him a call and tell him to help you with anything you need."

"Hey, what's up with that Tiffany Jones thing?" he added, trying to sound as if he were making small talk. "Was it as legit as the papers say?"

"As far as I know, there was no foul play. Just a freak, natural death. Anyway, the police don't know jack. Between you and me though, it seems a little suspicious. Keep your ears open. If you hear anything get back to me, all right."

"Bet," he said, "and you do the same. I ain't superstitious, but when a star big as Tiffany buys it for no apparent reason I get a little nervous. Then there was this airplane incident. Could be something is in the stars, you know what I'm saying."

"No, not really, sugar. But I'll definitely keep you up to date. Meanwhile, take it easy. What are the chances of lightning striking twice?" Kim laughed. When Ruff Daddy didn't answer for a full ten seconds, Kim continued. "Look, if you need some help closing that deal with the English dude, I can get a plane today. Things are slow."

"Naw, that's all right. I can handle it, you know that. Like Mo says, I'm probably being a little paranoid. I'll talk to you later."

Ruff Daddy shut down the phone and, after a short pause, turned back to Mo. "You still got heat?" he asked. "Don't try to take it through the metal detector, dawg."

"For real! I'm gon let Wardell take it back to Newark."

"On the bus?"

"Naw, let the nigger take a taxi."

"He in yo bank. It's yo gun," Ruff said.

Finally, Wardell returned with two first-class airline tickets to Atlanta. Mo gave him a wad of money, slipped him the gun, and then watched him go outside and get into a taxi.

"I wonder what the taxi driver gon say when Wardell tells him to go to Newark . . . New Jersey."

"I hope Wardell don't put yo gun to the guy's head and tell him he gotta go if he wants to or not."

When Mo and Ruff Daddy took their seats in the first-class section of Delta Flight 1720, there was an immediate buzz among the other passengers. Some quickly guessed that they were hip-hop artists or entrepreneurs. Besides the jewelry and attire, they carried themselves with a self-assured attitude that set them apart from the average passenger. Ruff Daddy ignored them, but he did notice that the Asian woman was also in first class and the Hispanic-looking dude was seated in coach.

Mo still didn't think they knew each other. When Ruff Daddy pointed it out to him, he grunted, "Naw, no way," and stretched out, taking full advantage of the spacious seat. "Now this is what I'm talkin' bout. You feel me, son?" he said.

"Got that right."

"When I was in Attica, I never thought I'd see daylight again, let alone fly first class."

"Yeah," Ruff Daddy said, "that's when I was in college."

"Hey, dawg, prison wasn't bad. You learned what you needed to know in college. I learned what I needed to know in prison and on the streets of Harlem working for Shabazz."

"You escaped, I dropped out. So did we learn enough?"

"We're in first class, ain't we."

The flight attendant came by flashing her blondes-have-more-fun smile. "Can I get you gentlemen a drink?"

Mo ordered Scotch. Ruff Daddy opened one eye and ordered club soda.

When the drinks arrived, Ruff Daddy lifted his glass in a toast. "This boy Brixton is hot," he said. "Definitely the stuff. You don't have to hide out to listen to it. It's street. You can pump it up. 'Til it hits big though, some people gonna be afraid of it—Beatles music in hip-hop," he laughed. "What's that about?"

"Running through Strawberry Fields forever with a AK-47."

"Naw, that ain't what this dude's rappin' about, you'll see."

Ruff Daddy placed his glass on the fold-down tray and settled back in his seat. We'll see, he thought as he closed his eyes.

Atlanta

Ruff Daddy was livid when he found that his personal driver, Candido, was not at the Hartsfield Atlanta International Airport to meet the flight. He had sent Candido ahead so they would have one of the company's three Lincoln Navigator stretches waiting for them. Instead they had to take a taxi, and Candido met them later in their suite at the Swissotel out on Peachtree Road, not far from the airport.

He told them that the police had stopped him in North Carolina. "They had me sitting out on the ground while they tore all the paneling out of the doors just looking for drugs."

"Shit, I don't mess with no drugs. They think any black dude with a car like that must be into drugs. Why didn't you call me on the cellphone?"

"I really thought I was going to be to the airport on time. I musta missed you guys by ten minutes. So I ran on over here to catch up with you to tell you in person what happened. They kept me four hours. I was cuffed in the police car. They was driving me toward town when they got a call that there was nothing found in the car and brought me back."

"How long was you away from the car?"

"'Bout two hours."

Ruff Daddy turned to Mo, who had already turned on the television set and ordered an X-rated movie.

"Hey, can't we take care of business before you get into that shit," he said. "There's an Atlanta detective named Freddy Carmichael, get him on the phone. Tell him I need him or an off-duty Atlanta cop to ride with us while I'm in town. I don't like this, something funny going

on here. I need to play this one cool. They might have planted something in the car and be just waiting to bust me for possession of what
they planted."

"Why would someone do that?" Mo asked.

"Look, just do what I say, nigga. You don't need to know everything."

"Yo, I didn't mean no harm, dawg. But you need to chill. You been
buggin' ever since we heard about that thing at the Apollo. What's up?
I'm 'spose to be yo chief of security. I need to know about all this.
What's going down, Ruff?"

"We'll talk later."

"Yo dawg, this is a fuckin' mess."

"All I know is these new Brixton tracks better be damn good. C'mon
Candido, I need to ride."

"Yo, you want me wid you?" Mo asked.

"Naw."

Downstairs, Ruff Daddy climbed into the Navigator and told Candido to drive, anywhere, it didn't matter. He trusted the security of a
cellphone more than he did the hotel phone, and he had to make
some calls. The first was to Dallas, and for two or three minutes he
spoke with K. J. Hunter about the deal they were involved in. When he
signed off, he seemed a little less tense. K. J. didn't seem to be sweating
a thing. He then tried calling Klaus Svrenson in New York, but got his
service instead. He hadn't talked to him since the night of Tiffany's
death; in fact, no one he knew had. That worried him.

Finally, he called Audrey Chung, the Chinese woman who ran his
office in New York. He affectionately called her "Assistant in Charge,"
since she was the only person in the world who knew all of his secrets.
She was the only person he trusted completely. Before meeting her he
had thought that loyalty was a fantasy. But she had taught him that it
could be real. She was absolutely loyal to the person she worked for,
and she worked for the person who offered the best deal, not just the
most money, but the environment that suited her best. Except for vari-

ous temporary workers and consultants, she was the only person he employed in the office. She answered after two rings. "RuffRoad Entertainment Enterprises," she said.

"Whatup dawg?" he said, before asking about the progress of ruff-road.com, the Web site he was having built. It was a perfect pretext for the unexpected call because she knew how concerned he was about the Web site. It was being designed to compete with thesource.com and vibe.com. It was going to be a central cog in his media empire, a Web site like no other, full of the hard-core hip-hop stuff that he wanted to take into cyberspace.

"Oh, it's you! Good. I'm so glad it's you."

She always seemed happy and relieved to hear from him. It was as if each time he called he reconnected her to the exotic world that he had initially brought her into. She loved hip-hop, and for five minutes or so they talked about what he was doing in Atlanta and how the site was coming along. Finally, Ruff Daddy broke off the conversation.

"Did you talk to Clarence?" he abruptly asked, referring to Clarence Johnson, the New York contact who worked on another of his projects.

"Yes, he checked in, everything is okay on his end."

"You're sure he didn't say anything about a problem?" he said.

"Absolutely sure."

"Perfect. Now you know why I love you. Anything else, any other calls, Klaus or Lester from Paris?"

"No, not a thing. Oh, wait, there was a strange call this morning from a guy who called himself John Williams. It was weird because he had a foreign accent. Definitely didn't sound like a John Williams. I checked caller I.D., but it was blocked."

"What did he want?"

"Well, he said it was urgent that he contact you. He even asked for your itinerary. I didn't give it to him, of course."

"That's my girl," he said after a pause. "I got to run. Talk to you later."

Ruff Daddy signed off and closed his eyes, deep in thought. He reassured himself that he had been careful not to say anything that might tip someone off or be used against him. Not in the Lincoln Navigator or on any unsecured phone. His office phone could be tapped and, who knows, maybe the cops had been only pretending to search the car. Maybe they were hiding a listening device. From what he'd been able to determine, no one had been harmed except Tiffany, and, according to Klaus and Kim, that may or may not have been anything but a diabetic seizure. Perhaps, as Mo had said, he was just being "par-a-noid." But John Williams. Who the hell was he? Paranoid or not, I got to watch it, he told himself.

"Candido, let's get back to the hotel," he said through the microphone that connected the back of the custom Lincoln to the shielded-off driver's seat.

New York City

Kim paced back and forth in front of the window of her office on 57th Street and Broadway. Below her, a panoramic view of Central Park opened up, lulling her with peaceful scenes of rolling meadows and lush, robust trees swaying in the summer breeze. From her corner office on the forty-second floor, Kim could see all the way uptown to Turtle Pond, with its stone castle perched at the edge of a towering bluff overlooking the water.

No matter how hectic things got, no matter how many inflated egos she had to soothe or how many impossible things her frivolous, pampered clients sometimes demanded, Kim could always lose herself staring out of her window at the breathtaking view of the park. Afterward, she was usually ready to face whatever challenge had been dumped at her feet.

But today seemed different. Kim felt as if she were off her game.

She was confused and unsettled. Luckily, she wasn't very busy. She'd been scheduled for all-day meetings negotiating film options for two of her clients. But one meeting had been canceled and the other postponed for a week. It was unusual that she had absolutely nothing to do.

On another day she would have welcomed the break in her grueling schedule. But the timing couldn't have been worse. Left to its own devices, Kim's mind played with her. The conversation with Ruff Daddy had reminded her of Tiffany lying on the floor with her eyes still wide open, and her makeup, so carefully and delicately applied, caking into a garish death mask.

The funeral was scheduled for 2 P.M. the next day. It would be a huge affair at the Abyssinian Baptist Church, with thousands of fans and admirers joining Tiffany's family and friends in mourning her passing. Kim had tried to call Klaus earlier to see if he wanted her help in arranging any of the details, but she hadn't been able to reach him.

She decided that now was a perfect time to try again.

Thankful to have something concrete to do, Kim strode around her wide mahogany desk, sat back in her plush black-leather chair, and grabbed the phone. She dialed Klaus on his private line at home, thinking that that would be the easiest way to catch him.

The phone rang five times before a woman's voice came on the line and instructed her to leave a message.

That was strange. Even if Klaus wasn't taking any calls, his personal assistant Denise always picked up the line, usually before the second ring. Kim didn't want to start worrying over nothing, but this was strange. Where was he?

That thought made her remember that she'd also planned to call Tiffany's personal assistant Maria. Kim flipped open her Palm Pilot and scrolled to Maria's name. Maria lived with her mother and younger sister in an apartment up in Washington Heights.

Someone picked up the phone almost before Kim heard it start ringing and said, "Hola?"

"Good morning," Kim said. "I'm looking for Maria Casells."

"Who is this?" the woman asked in a heavily accented voice.

"This is Kim, Kim Carlyle—I was Tiffany Jones's manager. Rita . . . is that you?"

"Oh. Si, Miss Carlyle. It's me. I'm sorry. I thought I recognized your voice, but I wasn't sure."

"Rita, I'm looking for your sister. I haven't seen her since the other night and I wanted to make sure that she's okay."

"Maria's gone, Miss Carlyle."

"Gone? What do you mean?"

"She's gone. She left the country and said she was going home."

"But when? Why so suddenly?"

"I don't know, Miss Carlyle," Rita said. "We were surprised too. I actually thought you might be her calling to tell us where she's staying. We called my dad's family in Santo Domingo but she hasn't shown up there and my mom's family hasn't seen her yet either. Me and my mom, we're getting worried."

"When did she leave?" Kim asked.

"The morning after Tiffany died, God rest her soul. She said she had gotten a hold of some money and she was going to use it to go away because the reporters were too much. The phone didn't stop ringing that night or the next day. They kept trying to say things about my sister that weren't true."

"You haven't heard from her since?"

"No. Nothing. If she gets in touch with you, will you ask her to call us? My mother isn't handling this too well. She's scared now."

"Of course, Rita. Anything I hear, I'll let you know immediately."

Kim hung up the phone feeling more uneasy than before. It made sense that a shy, sensitive girl like Maria would run from the unwanted spotlight. But why wouldn't she tell her family where she was? It didn't add up.

As she sat with her hand resting on the receiver, the phone rang again. She glanced over at the caller I.D.; it was Universal Studios.

So much for having nothing to do.

Atlanta

Although he wasn't certain of any immediate danger, Ruff Daddy decided to change his schedule. If anyone had found out where he was supposed to be, changing the schedule might throw them off. The plan wasn't foolproof because, besides Audrey Chung and, maybe, Mo, he wasn't certain he could trust anybody. Instead of waiting until after the concert to talk to Brixton, at 7 P.M. he went unannounced to the Westin Peachtree Plaza where the rapper was staying.

Brixton agreed to join Ruff and his posse, and make a quick trip to the in-home studio of one of Ruff Daddy's friends, where they could listen to more of Brixton's demo tracks.

Candido drove the Lincoln Navigator. Sitting with him in the front passenger's seat was Freddy Carmichael, the off-duty Atlanta detective referred by Kim. They had decided to celebrate and party a little, so they brought Lil' Luv, a voluptuous dark-skinned exotic dancer with a very flattering short blond bush-baby hairdo. She sat in the second row of seats.

As the only female in the posse she had already made it known that she was "down for whatever with whoever." Brixton and Mo sat on either side of her, talking across her.

"Hey, you know it's funny," Mo shouted above the sound of Dr. Dre's "Rat-tat-tat-tat, late at night with my gat" coming from the CD player. "I can't help it. Every time they tell me some dude is British, I expect to see a little fem white guy, and then we roll up on a big black nigga like you with a British accent."

"I love the way you talk," Lil' Luv said, grinning to show off her gold-capped tooth, which matched her gold nose ring and gold tongue ring.

Ruff Daddy sat silently in the third row of seats. He listened to the conversation, but his mind was elsewhere. What had really happened to Tiffany, and where the hell was Klaus? Was the forced landing in Baltimore of his lease jet just an accident? Who was John Williams? Were the guys in North Carolina really cops? His mind was racing with unanswered questions.

Ruff Daddy stared out of the window trying to come up with answers when suddenly the deafening sound of real gunfire and shattered glass and metal exploded in his ears. Candido ducked and swerved the Lincoln across on-coming traffic to escape the Jeep that had pulled alongside them. Before Ruff ducked he saw what looked like a Mac-10 submachine gun and an AK-47 assault rifle belching fire from the window of the Jeep.

Both Freddy Carmichael and Mo Hump drew their guns, but by the time the Lincoln came to a halt the Jeep had sped away. Candido had sideswiped two vehicles before he pulled the SUV to the curb on the other side of Piedmont Avenue. Lil' Luv started screaming when she saw that Mo Hump was bleeding from an arm wound and Brixton's head had nearly been severed from his body.

FOUR

K. J. Hunter insisted that he had been involved with only one foreigner—Brigette Nguyen. Of course being from South Texas that did not include "Wets," or "Wetbacks," as Mexicans were called by the locals. They were called Wets because, according to the widely held view, most of them had, or their parents had, waded across the Rio Grande to get into the United States. Still, they were not considered foreigners; there were too many of them and, by now, more than a few had genuine Texan blood. The way K. J. saw it, Brigette was his first foreigner, even though he'd slept with plenty of Wets since his high-school days.

On the morning of the Lone Star Jewelry Show and Diamond Expo International, K. J. was busily working the phone as he waited for Brigette. He called her the "little Korean," even though she was from Vietnam and really wasn't that small. Subtle distinctions didn't mean much to him. To him she was just a hot little yellowish-brown woman whose country the U.S. of A. had once been at war with back before he was born. When he met her four months ago, he had only been interested in sleeping with her. But once he discovered she knew more about diamonds than he did, he brought her into the business. It was a perfect arrangement; her work was more than satisfactory on every level.

K. J. was only twenty-seven but he was a self-made millionaire, with, of course, the help that his family's oil industry millions gave him. But it had been almost two years since he dipped into the family vault. He had his own fortune now, and it was growing every day. The 2001 drop in the market had barely fazed him since he never had any faith in trendy high-tech stocks and had sold the few he owned before the crash on the advice of his brother, Bryan, a lawyer with deep Wall Street connections. He had learned to stick to the basics with stock investments, which for a Texan meant oil and cattle. But he also had the instincts and unblinking gall of a crafty, frontier-town saloon gambler. And of late it was his proprietorship in the gemstone business and major holding in a national mortuary company with funeral homes in thirty-two states, a doubly profitable enterprise, that were the sources of his quickly accrued capital. In addition, he owned a booming Dallas-based luxury used-car dealership that was a consistent money-maker.

He was thinking about Brigette as he sat on the side of his bed at the Fairmont, a four-star, European-style, twenty-five-story hotel located in the Dallas Arts District. The Fairmont was the best that a cowboy town like Dallas could come to mustering a London/Paris flavor.

The district surrounding the Fairmont was touted as the largest urban cultural district in the nation. It was dotted with galleries, theaters, performing and visual arts schools, art museums, and the Meyerson Symphony Center, where cowboys, trying to acquire a taste for Bach and Beethoven, often fell asleep listening to the Dallas Symphony Orchestra. On a few occasions, K. J. himself had been coerced into showing up at Symphony Center and listening to what he scornfully called "operatic music."

He joked that they called it operatic music because it was the kind of music they played in a hospital operating room when you were brought in to be patched up after a gunshot wound or a snakebite.

Dressed only in silk boxer shorts, a Stetson hat, and $600 Lucchese calfskin cowboy boots, K. J. Hunter picked up the phone and gazed out at the impressive skyline of downtown Dallas. *Forbes* magazine had cited it as one of the "Best Cities for Business" in the United States, and K. J. had taken full advantage of the city and his substantial connections. In Dallas, K. J. ruled.

Smiling, he dialed up his old friend Billy Ray Farley. His secretary said, "Hold on a minute, Mr. Hunter, he'll be right with you." Three minutes passed. K. J. thought Billy Ray was keeping him waiting intentionally. Bastard!

Suddenly Bill Ray's voice boomed through the phone "K. J., how are you?"

"Never mind how I am. What the hell took you so long and do we have a deal or not?"

"Sorry 'bout that, K. J., I was on the line to New York." Billy Ray was speaking from his office atop the Bank of America Tower in downtown Dallas. "Yeah, of course the deal is on!"

"Then where the hell is the delivery?"

"It's on the way, K. J."

"If I don't see the goodies soon I want my damn money back." K. J. used the term "goodies" in telephone conversations to refer to anything that was being delivered to him. It was a well-ingrained precaution. He didn't want the Feds snooping into the affairs of an enterprising businessman like himself. Not that he was dealing with illegal goods. While he seldom turned down a lucrative deal and occasionally slipped over the line, he usually traded in perfectly legal commodities—spot oil, Arabian and thoroughbred horses, precious metals, gemstones, art objects, antique cars, cash. It was the source of origin and his "alternative" means of distribution that were sometimes questionable.

"K. J., I told you I already advanced the cash. I can't give you your money back."

"Take it out of your pocket or I'll take it out of your hide, but I want my damn money back if I don't see all the goodies by next week Friday."

"K. J., I told you, the deal's in the works. We've got to wait for someone to die."

"Goddamn it, Billy Ray, people die every day."

"Were waiting for someone to die in Europe."

"People are dying in Europe every day, Billy Ray, don't trifle with me. I'm not a man to be trifled with."

"Did the Vietnamese dame get there?"

"Oh, is that what she is? I thought she was Korean."

"Damn, K. J., you're screwin' her, you should at least know what country she comes from."

"Why?" K. J. laughed for the first time.

"One of these days your sex life is going to get you killed," Billy Ray said. "You always was a crude bastard. That's what's wrong with you."

"Listen, Billy Ray, ain't a goddamn thing wrong with me except I want the goodies. I want 'em PDQ, you understand!"

"Next week."

"Next week! I ought a come over there and pistol whip your butt all up and down the expressway, boy. Goddamn, you piss me off Billy Ray."

Billy Ray didn't react to the mock threat since he and K. J. had been friends since high school. They had played football at A&M together, and besides, in Texas Billy Ray was nearly as powerful as K.J.

"How 'bout the colored boy?" Billy Ray asked. "Where is he?"

"Ruff Daddy? I like that boy. He may be the only straight shooter in the goddamn bunch. Yo! Old buddy, there's someone at the door.

Probably the Korean. Friday week? Goddamn, boy. Okay, Friday week, that's when you get your ass kicked if I don't have my goodies." He hung up. Just as K. J. headed for the door the phone in his hand rang. "K. J. Hunter here," he said.

"Yo! K. J., this is Ruff Daddy."

"Yo! Ruff Daddy, old buddy. How's the hop-hip business? I thought you was gonna send me some of those hip-hop CDs. Oh, man, man! I heard about that thing in Atlanta. You all right?" K. J. swung open the door, reached out, picked Brigette up in his arms, and carried her into the room as if she were a nine- or ten-year-old child.

"Yeah, I'm cool. I've taken necessary precautions," he said, before pausing. "What the fuck is going on there? You got someone with you?"

"Yeah," he laughed, kissing Brigette as he carried her toward the bed. "She's one of my finest associates."

"Shit, man, you know I don't discuss no business when a third party's present."

"Hold on, old buddy, this ain't no third party. She's part of the deal—in more ways than one." Brigette nibbled at K. J.'s ear as he listened to Ruff Daddy.

"Yeah, if you say so, but get the bitch away from the phone. I ain't broadcasting my conversation—not after the call from New York and the Atlanta deal. I don't know who's watching or listening. I don't trust nobody."

Hunter sat Brigette down on the bed.

"What about you," Ruff Daddy said, "you noticed anybody on your tail?"

"No way, not a soul," K. J. laughed. "Ain't nobody gonna fuck with me in Texas. They don't wanna mess with a good ole boy—not down here."

"Don't let ya head get too big for that ten-gallon hat. Something's up, you better watch your ass."

"Yo, where are you?"

"Never mind that. I'm calling to let you know the deal is on. I'll call Billy Ray when we're through."

"Great, great, he's waiting for the word."

"You got enough merchandise for the show right now?"

"Sure, but I need more for the Houston show. I like to have it in hand in advance. I don't like foul-ups. It takes a lot of money to put these shows together."

"The material is moving."

"Great. You just saved Billy Ray an ass kicking, for real," K. J. laughed. "Say, what really happened in Atlanta? The only word I got was what I read in the papers. You gotta fill me in—wait, there's another call coming in. How can I get back to you?"

"I'll call you," Ruff Daddy said before hanging up.

"Yeah, it's me!" K. J. yelled into the phone, then immediately changed his tone. It was his wife, calling from Fort Worth. "Hey, sweetheart. I was just thinking about you."

"I bet you were, K. J. I just bet you were just thinking about me so much that you didn't call home this morning like you said you would." K. J.'s wife, a former high-school cheerleader, was not unaware of his philandering.

Brigette stood up. Holding his hand over the receiver, K. J. told her he would meet her in the ballroom at the exhibition. He patted her bottom as she left.

"Yup, well, I can explain that, darling," he said to his wife. "I know, I know."

When K. J. finally arrived at the Lone Star Jewelry Show, he was doubly agitated. Not only was Ruff Daddy acting a little strange, but his true-blue, American-as-apple-pie wife was getting frisky and had threatened to leave him and go home to her daddy.

K. J. stood in the center of the ballroom under a huge neon sign blinking DIAMONDS FOREVER and looked out over the vast array of booths. Buyers packed the huge trade-show floor, flitting from booth to booth to peruse the glistening showcases where diamonds, gemstones, and designer jewelry of every sort were on display. He knew he could patch things up with his wife—a little trinket, some piece of jewelry would do that. But the other thing, the shooting in Atlanta. What was that about? Did Ruff Daddy know more than he was saying? As soon as the show closed he'd have to look into it. For now it had to be strictly business.

Hundreds of diamond wholesalers and exhibitors had turned out for the show. They had come from nearly every corner of the globe— Belgium, China, France, Germany, Great Britain, Greece, Hong Kong, Ireland, Israel, Italy, Japan, Singapore, Spain, Sri Lanka, Switzerland, South Africa, Tahiti, Thailand, and more—to display their wares. Three of the booths were selling gems that belonged to him and his associates—rough diamonds that would net nearly $6 million. That thought set his heart pumping nearly as fast as watching a corral full of fine thoroughbred stallions. But it was not, as some suspected, the money that excited him. He already had plenty of that. No, it was the wrangling, the careful planning, the shrewd manipulations, and the precise execution that went into the deal. The danger! For K. J. there was nothing like it; except maybe riding and breaking one of his high-spirited stallions.

Trying to relax, K. J. wandered through the maze of exhibits until he found Brigette. "Sorry 'bout the interruption, but we'll have plenty of time later," he said.

She smiled and surreptitiously touched his hand. "Everything all right?"

"Nothing a Texan can't handle," he said. "Let's go over and see how the goods are moving."

They pushed their way through the crowd as the sensuous Texas drawl of the show's pitchwoman oozed from loudspeakers, describing current trends and luring buyers with special offers.

"Designers are making a big to-do over burnt oranges and yellows, or earthy browns and lush greens as design elements in apparel and accessory fashion trends. Jewelers are responding by making statements with pink stones ranging from intense, magenta rhodolite garnets and rubellite tourmalines through a wide palette of lighter tourmalines and pale pink sapphires—beautiful! So beautiful! Watch out for . . ."

"K. J.! K. J.! You old horse thief," someone shouted.

K. J. turned to see a small man with wrinkled, weather-beaten skin advancing toward him. "Clyde! Hey, keep that horse thief stuff quiet, partner," K. J. said, smiling broadly. "People might take you serious." He grabbed the man's hand and shook it vigorously. "What are you doing here?"

Clyde T. Hammond, despite his harmless avuncular look, was an oil pipeline manufacturer and old friend of K. J.'s father who had connections that stretched from the White House to the Middle East and, rumor had it, to the inner circles of America's underworld Eastern mob. He laughed now and, stepping back, squared off in a boxer's stance and threw a few blows into K. J.'s midsection.

"Still tight as a drum," K. J. said as he permitted the old man to hit him hard in the abdomen.

"Just out for a breath of fresh air," Clyde said.

"More perfume in the air in here than stinky stuff at a skunk's picnic."

"Hey, come on, take a walk with me back toward the antique and estate jewelry pavilion."

"Ah . . . look Brigette, I'll be right back. Don't go anywhere, we have some unfinished business."

"One of your wild horses couldn't drag me away," she said as the two men left.

"What's a matter. You fall on hard times, Winston? Got to sell the family heirlooms?"

"No. Actually, son, I came down here to talk to you. I knew I'd find you here. Your mother's worried and so is your dad."

"About what, Clyde?" K. J. paused to survey the old man's face. "About what?"

"Let's step over here," Clyde said, pointing to a quiet area near a bank of telephones. "Conflict diamonds. They think you're trading in diamonds that come from one of them African countries where they're having civil wars."

"What in the world are you talking about, Clyde?"

"Blood diamonds, boy, that's what they call 'em. That whole business stinks to high heaven."

"What's that got to do with me?"

"Terrible things are going on, K. J., folks cutting off the hands of children in Sierra Leone and Angola. You must know the rebels are using money from illegal diamonds to buy weapons."

"Tell me, Winston, what is an illegal diamond? Diamonds are perfectly legal. And since when did you start caring—"

"You know damn well what I mean. They're trying to pass a bill in Congress banning the import of them diamonds, right now."

"Yeah, well, until the bill passes, the diamonds aren't banned, am I right? And since when did Daddy start caring about Africa and the Third World? I really don't need a lecture about clean diamonds from him or you. You and I both know there's plenty of dirt in every business—even the oil business, the one you and Daddy are in."

"Your mother and—"

"You know, Clyde," K. J. snapped, staring at the old man suspiciously, "I don't think you even talked to them about it. My daddy would've called me if he was really concerned. He sure wouldn't have sent somebody like you. The Hunters keep family matters in the family. What's the deal, Clyde? What in hell are you up to?"

"You don't have no reason to talk to me like that, boy. It's pretty simple, let's just say I'm trying to warn you to get out of the creek before the dam breaks."

"Look, old man, your concern is touching, but knowing what I know about your business, I wouldn't believe you if you had your damn tongue notarized. You haven't lifted a hand to help anybody, including my daddy, since I've known you. Not unless there was something in it for you."

"Let's not get personal, my boy," Clyde said. "But if you know me so well, then you know that I've got as many connections as you and your daddy. You may think you've got everything in hand, but there's some stuff happening now that you ain't even considered. Whether you know it or not, you could use some help, and I'm the man that can supply it."

"Is that a threat, Clyde? You about to drop a dime on me? Or are you just fishing and hoping to buy into something that you don't know shit about?"

"You was always a clever boy, K. J. You figure it out. But as an old friend of the family, I'm telling you to watch your back. You're dealing with some ruthless folks. Your daddy and your highfalutin' lawyer brother ain't gonna be able to protect you. I'm not even sure that I can."

"Spit it out, Winston. What are you—"

"Stay clear of the Vietnamese girl. I'm just warning you for your family's sake—especially with your brother planning to run for governor some day, and maybe even the Senate. If anything blows up, everybody is going to get hurt. You don't have to admit it or deny it, all I come to say is that folks are worried and some folks are hoppin' mad."

"You know, I don't think anybody's worried except you, and I'm not falling for your scam. My business is my own, and I'm advising you to stay out of it."

Clyde started to speak again, but before he could utter another word, K. J. turned and abruptly stormed away, leaving the old man standing alone. As far as K. J. could see, there was no need to continue the conversation. He was convinced it was a shakedown and, until he discovered exactly what the old man knew, he wasn't saying anything else. Klaus had been evasive, but he had warned him that things might get sticky. Still, K. J. hadn't expected it to happen this quickly. He had also been told not to panic — just wait and ride it out. But with Clyde sniffing at his heels, he felt he had to do something. At least get on a secure phone, make some calls, and attempt to protect himself. For that, he couldn't return to his ranch. He had to get to his hideaway, the condo he kept under an assumed name in Arlington for anonymous trysts or just to cool out and disappear. With the exception of Sally Brierton, the cute cocktail waitress he picked up at Avanti, and a few high-class call girls, no one even knew he owned it.

K. J. was headed toward the exit when Brigette intercepted him. "What's the hurry?" she asked. "You look like you've just seen a ghost. Anyway, I thought we were going to get together later."

"We'll have to take a rain check; something unexpected has come up. I have to leave." He pulled away from her and started toward the door, then, thinking about their earlier foreplay, turned back. "You know, you could come with me. After this is settled, I'll need some TLC."

"I'd love to," she said, "but I have to get back to the booth. I'm talking to a buyer. Besides, don't you think one of us should stay here and keep an eye on the goods? Why don't you call me when you get on the road — we'll arrange something for later."

"Sounds like a plan, honey. See you later."

K. J. hurried to the check-out desk, tossed his room key at the clerk, and told her to check him out of his room and put the bill on his tab. "And buzz valet parking, have them bring my car around," he said, striding toward the entrance.

Outside, he paced nervously as he waited for the car. He wasn't sure how he would solve this, but he knew he had to get back to Klaus and find out more. If that didn't work, he'd have to go even higher. He felt that he'd been played into a corner without wiggle room, but he was sure he'd survive. Ever since his college days on the football field, he'd managed to find a way to get over no matter what the odds were. This was no different, he told himself.

The green Porsche screeched to a halt in front of the hotel and a pimple-faced teenager stepped out smiling as if he'd just been to Disneyland. K. J. sneered at him but still slapped a ten-dollar bill in his hand before sliding into the driver's seat. He had just bought the Porsche to replace his year-old Ferrari, and he didn't appreciate the way the kid handled it. He lit a Cuban cigar before angrily pulling away from the hotel onto Akard Street.

"Damn Germans just make a more reliable car than the Italians," he said aloud when he finally steered the green beauty out onto Interstate 30 and headed west toward his Arlington retreat. The rush of afternoon air, warm but dry, and sight of the long, flat expanse of highway ahead, eased his tension a bit, so, despite his problems, he decided that seeing Brigette later was not a bad idea.

As he shifted into fifth gear and eased the speedometer up past seventy miles per hour, he reached into the glove compartment for his cellphone. The car had just reached eighty when he pressed the talk button and dialed Brigette's number. The phone rang twice before he heard a loud popping noise underneath the car. Instinctively he pressed his foot to the brake, then began frantically pumping them when the car didn't respond. Before he could swerve to avoid the collision, the Porsche slammed into the back of the slower-moving U-Haul truck ahead of him. The truck was driven twenty-five yards before it came to a halt with the totaled sports car buried in its rear end.

FIVE

WASHINGTON, D.C. — THURSDAY, JULY 19

Congressman Dave Hamlin (R-Idaho) stood in front of the wide, triple-paneled mirror in the immaculate art deco men's room at Georgia Brown's, the upscale soul-food restaurant on 15th Street in downtown Washington. As the elected representative of the Second Congressional District in Idaho, Hamlin was a first-term congressman. In most Washington circles, he was both an anomaly and a curiosity. And for many members of the Congressional Black Caucus he was an embarrassment. The Caucus, however, had little choice in accepting him. He was, after all, black, or, as he insisted, brown.

Staring into the mirror now, his reflection appeared blurry and distorted, and he wavered unsteadily as he blinked his eyes and leaned closer to the crystal-clear glass. He was drunk. Smiling, he peered at his image, and in a deep baritone voice intoned, "My fellow . . . Americans." He repeated the phrase several times and laughed as the sound echoed throughout the empty room.

"My fellow Americans," he began again, "I come before you to stand behind you . . . to tell you something you already know."

Then, straightening his black bow tie and adjusting the lapels of his tux, his expression shifted. He thought of all the occasions when he had been and would again have to be perfectly serious despite having had a few too many cocktails. He pulled his shoulders back, drew himself up to his full height of five-seven, and set his round, bloated face in a mask of statesmanlike propriety. "My fellow Americans, I come before you tonight, at this historic juncture in our great nation's political life, to announce my candidacy for president of the United States. I am deeply humbled by your unwavering support. . . ."

He smiled at the authoritative timbre of his voice, the ease with which he could shift and project deep sincerity even when, as now, he was thoroughly intoxicated. And if things kept going his way, he might have to speak to the American people in exactly that manner. Congressman Dave Hamlin was convinced that he had been chosen to undertake the historic journey that had started back with his election as the first and only African American ever to be elected president of a senior class at Mountain View High School in Twin Falls, Idaho.

Today that journey had been fueled considerably. Earlier in the day an aide had informed him that his support for the current farm subsidies bill had elicited a huge contribution to his political action committee by the owners of a major midwestern agricultural cartel. The beauty of his position was that the general public would applaud him for supporting the nation's small-farm owners. It couldn't be better, he thought; he was indeed blessed. Yes, throughout his life, doing the right thing had been extremely profitable for him. And, except for the unsettling call from New York City four days ago, even the FBI or the CIA could not have found a happier, more self-satisfied American than thirty-nine-year-old Dave Hamlin.

Dave Hamlin was a marvel in American politics, having been elected to Congress from a district that had a white population of 472,644, and an African American population of only 2,258, or about 5 percent. There were also ten times as many Hispanics, three times as many Indians and Eskimos, and twice as many Pacific Islanders and Asians as blacks. Hamlin, in fact, was married to a Native American woman and had three teenage children by her. His family had remained in Twin Falls, and here in Washington he was enjoying his freedom and status as the representative of his diverse constituency. It was quite a feat for a small-town boy whose classmates had begun calling him "Tater" in high school.

They had meant it derisively, noting that he was about the same color as an Idaho spud. And, when he squinted, they said, his head resembled one—a cheerful, smiling tuber shaded by a ring of close-cropped curly hair. The name had stuck through high school and college, where he had been a star in track and football at the University of Idaho. And now, without knowing about its school days origin, some of his colleagues, including members of the Black Caucus, also used the name, but only behind his back. Dave Hamlin didn't mind—not at all.

He had accepted it good-naturedly in high school and later, when he ran for office, embraced it. He had discovered that public humility, even if you didn't mean it, was very attractive to voters. And if you were from Idaho, what better nickname than "Tater." But beneath the jolly, self-effacing demeanor, Hamlin was as ambitious and slick as any politician in Washington.

He was still smiling broadly as he returned to his table, noting the chest-high curling cherry-wood partitions that divided the room and the sculpted bronze ribbonlike ornaments suspended from the ceiling. His date, Christine Spivey, pulled his chair away from the table so he could sit. A large, luscious, butter-colored woman with lots of red makeup and thin black eyelashes, the thirty-one-year-old lobbyist had been appointed the task of getting close to the new Idaho congressman and of making sure he met some like-minded people among Washington's elite.

"I just love this place. I just love it," he gushed to his dinner companions. At the table were Senator Ray "Pancho" Hernandez (R-Texas), Congressman John Durham (R-Pennsylvania), and their wives. It was Hamlin's first visit to Georgia Brown's, and he was thoroughly impressed. They had come to the elegant restaurant after leaving a giant Republican fund-raiser at the Omni-Shoreham Hotel where none other than President George W. Bush put his hand on Hamlin's shoulder and said: "We're counting on great things from you."

Hamlin had flashed his reassuring don't-worry-I'm-your-boy smile at the president and winked, which led "Dubya" to pause and note that Tater was the kind of American he could count on.

Now Hamlin smugly scanned the menu in front of him. He had thought of soul food as simple fare, collard greens, chitlins, corn bread, ham hocks, and such, but the menu here was as sophisticated as the decor. He considered the overall possibilities but finally chose horseradish- and peppercorn-crusted filet mignon with pan-bronzed scallops, whipped potatoes, and spinach. Wow! he thought. Putting the menu aside, he sat back and surveyed the well-heeled, multi-ethnic crowd that surrounded them as the others ordered.

When the waiter left, Christine Spivey, Rowena Hernandez, and Connie Durham excused themselves to go to the ladies' room. Hamlin watched Spivey's sensual walk and he thought of the trucks that he sometimes saw on highways with a WIDE LOAD sign across the back. Her hips moved fluidly beneath the silk fabric of her tightly fitted, flowered evening dress. Yes, indeed, he thought, this night looked very promising.

Spivey stopped and spoke to several patrons, introducing her companions, as they strolled through the restaurant. She was well known among Washington politicos and special-interest groups. Not only did she know where many of the capital's skeletons were hidden, but she also knew how to connect people with the people they needed to know, which meant that she needed to know everyone who was anyone in the town. And tonight, as usual, she was busily working the floor.

Just before entering the rest room, Spivey excused herself from the congressmen's wives. She called her boss, the lobbyist Emanuel Epstein, on her cellphone, and informed him that both Durham and Hamlin were in pocket to support the diamond embargo bill. "In fact, they've both promised Representative Tony Hall that he can count on them," she said. "But it's going to take more than I have to offer to get Hernandez's support for the trade sanctions bill."

"What's Hernandez's problem?" Epstein asked as he paced impatiently across his suite at the Watergate Hotel. "What do you think it'll take?"

"Don't worry," Spivey said, "I'll figure it out."

Back at the table, Dave Hamlin was involved in a lively conversation with Durham and Hernandez. He looked up when a tall, elegant man with smooth ink-black skin passed and tapped him on his shoulder. It was the controversial Sierra Leone businessman, Ezekiel Kwabena. He wore a colorfully embroidered, silk kaftan over neatly pressed trousers and a white shirt and tie. When he took a seat at a table near the rear of the restaurant, his piercing eyes and toothy, milk-white smile were directed at Hamlin. Within minutes, the congressman rose and went over to greet Kwabena. After a brief discussion, he and Kwabena returned to the table where Hernandez and Durham were seated.

"Ambassador Kwabena, I'd like you to meet Congressman John Durham of Pennsylvania and Senator Ray Hernandez of South Texas."

"Pleased to meet you," the African said, flashing a broad, clever smile.

"I've been talking to the congressman and the senator about the grave import of the house action relating to the diamond trade, Ambassador," Hamlin said, assuming a solemn air. He called Kwabena ambassador even though he knew he wasn't the country's official representative. In fact, the businessman was more influential than the ambassador. He had connections that extended from oil- and diamond-field power brokers to the highest corridors of the presidential palace.

"Good! Good! We must have a concerted effort," Kwabena said, extending his hand as Durham and Hernandez rose to greet him.

"I have been telling these gentlemen that we must take a stance that ends the misappropriation of funds by rebel forces in neighboring countries yet preserves the legitimacy of Sierra Leone's diamond trade on the international market," Hamlin said. "We need to get on the right side of this issue. A general boycott of the diamonds or even hasty legislation that usurps the country's involvement in the certification of its own resources would seriously undermine the sovereignty of the nation. I've assured Ambassador Kwabena that our aim is to stop the mayhem without jeopardizing the independence of his nation." Hamlin flashed a conspiratorial smile at Kwabena before turning back to Hernandez and Durham. "I'm sure you gentlemen agree."

"The brutality is unfortunate," Kwabena said. "It has left a distorted image of our country when, in fact, it is the—"

Seeing that the African was about to launch into a tirade, Hamlin interrupted him. "The bill in Congress now," he said, "would require importers to provide certification of origin for rough or polished diamonds before they can be sold in the U.S. But, as written now, it would place Sierra Leone's fate squarely in the hands of De Beers, the conglomerate which controls the world's diamond production, and the Belgian Diamond High Council, an organization whose past record with respect to sanctioning illegal African diamonds is, at best, questionable. In effect, gentlemen, we would be imposing a kind of economic colonial rule over the duly elected officials of Africa's free nations. And that is a situation we must avoid at all costs. No, I am convinced that we should seek a less politically damaging solution to this situation."

Hamlin looked at his colleagues expectantly.

"Well . . . I, uh, I of course favor an approach in which the diamond industry becomes involved in rallying public support for the fight against rebel factions and the wholesale slaughter of civilians," Hernandez said finally. "Otherwise there is a risk of backlash among Americans who buy about fifty percent of the world's diamond production. Still, I'm not sure of the government's proper role here."

"But Ray, I think the government must take the lead here," Hamlin said. "We must set a course that eliminates the unlawful sale of illegally obtained diamonds by the rebels and, at the same time, protect the independence of Sierra Leone."

"I certainly agree about the rightness of the cause," Hernandez said. "But achieving those ends may be more, well, complicated than you suspect, *Ambassador* Kwabena."

"I'll leave my card with both you and Congressman Durham," Kwabena said. "Give me a call, I'm sure I can satisfy your concerns." He shook their hands and smiled knowingly at Hernandez and Durham before walking back toward his table with Hamlin.

"Did you get a call from Klaus Svrenson?" Hamlin whispered.

"Yes, I did," Kwabena said, "and I see that he called you also." Suddenly a look of grave concern swept across his face. "What do you make of it?"

"Well, from what I understand from other sources, some *internal* house cleaning became necessary. Klaus, of course, was incensed by the death of his wife. Still, business is business," Hamlin said, glancing back toward his own table. "But I'm sure the matter has been cleared up with the incidents in Amsterdam and Dallas."

"I hope you're right. That responsibility, of course, lies with your colleagues in Europe and the States. In Freetown, betrayal or bungling resulting from greed is not tolerated. The situation would have been quickly dispatched. As it is, I've had some explaining to do," Kwabena said. "It would be unfortunate if I'm forced to turn elsewhere to assure the continuation of this arrangement."

"That won't be necessary."

"Good, but let's talk about it at another time. This is hardly the place to discuss . . . business," Kwabena said. Hamlin returned to his table.

Dave Hamlin rose and held the chair for Spivey when she returned from the ladies' room with the two other women.

"You're so sweet," she said.

"My pleasure," he said as the other two men stood up to seat their wives.

During dinner, Hamlin was generally unaware of anything in the restaurant except the delicious food on his plate and the equally delicious Christine Spivey, who occasionally rubbed her leg against his and smiled as she devoured the grilled catfish and black-eyed peas that she had ordered. He chatted with his dinner guests, occasionally shot a glance at Kwabena to see what he was up to, and, from time to time, smiled lecherously at Spivey. He also took note of the Hispanic man wearing sneakers and a running suit who paused as he passed their table. Hamlin had noticed him at the bar earlier when he sat with an Italian or Hispanic woman who was absolutely gorgeous.

"How did they let someone in a place like this with sneakers on?" He nodded toward the guy's feet.

"Those aren't just sneakers," Spivey said. "They're Kobe Adidas, darling, one hundred and fifty dollars, and the Men's Basketball Elevation Suit is one hundred and twenty-five."

"For a jump suit?" Durham asked as he swallowed his broccoli without chewing it. They all laughed, and Hamlin turned back to what was left of his meal.

During dessert and coffee, the three politicians talked about various concerns of the Republican Party. It was after eleven o'clock when Hamlin picked up the check and they left the restaurant. Outside, after the senator, the congressman, and their wives had gone, Hamlin leaned over and whispered into Spivey's ear. "Why, Tater," she gushed coyly, before she stepped forward and kissed him. He led her to his blue Lexus LS400.

Hamlin rubbed Spivey's butter-colored knee as they drove up Connecticut Avenue, with its large, stately red-brick homes. When they turned onto Nebraska Avenue and headed toward Military Road, he was imagining an evening of pleasure.

Spivey moved closer and rested her head on his shoulder as they cruised through the darkened streets. She was perfectly willing to spend the evening with Hamlin if that's what it took to establish herself as a confidant, someone who could influence him and the way he voted. Besides, although he sometimes played the fool, Hamlin was fast becoming an influential representative. And nothing attracted Spivey more than power.

This is what it's all about, Hamlin thought to himself. During his campaign, he had imagined what it would be like to really enjoy the spoils of American political life. And since he'd been in office, he'd taken full advantage of the situation. He was already amassing enough "contributions" and future "campaign funds" to ensure his reelection in five years. He laughed to himself, thinking about the diamond deal. It was sweet. And after that the sky was the limit. Why not run for president? If Jesse Jackson could do it, why not he. Even the Reverend Al Sharpton had announced that he was considering running for the White House. "You know this idea that black folk got that white folk won't elect a black person president is absolutely wrong," he said aloud.

"I agree, I agree," Spivey said. She smiled at him, pointing out directions as he drove.

"Things are changing," he said. "They appointed Clarence

Thomas to the Supreme Court, didn't they? Why not a black chief of state? I know I'm smart enough to be president."

"You got my vote," Spivey said, and kissed him gently on the cheek.

"You know I won my seat in Congress with sixty-four percent of the white vote," he said. "And that was despite the opposition of all the hate groups and militia groups in Idaho. Every time one of those suckers spoke out against me, I gained another few points in the polls."

"How'd you do with black voters?" Spivey asked, indicating that he should take the next turn onto the Rock Creek Parkway.

"Slightly better, actually, around seventy-two percent. You don't have to sell out your people to get white votes," he said defensively. "This is what the Twin Falls newspaper had to say about me. I know it by heart. 'Dave Hamlin parts company with black voters on many key civil rights issues but he wins black votes because of the force and sincerity of his convictions and genuine down-home charm.' The editorial went on to praise my 'courageous, hard-nose approach to affirmative action' and ended by saying that 'black voters realize that Dave Hamlin represents a forward-looking approach to racial issues, not one that whines over our society's past transgressions. Mr. Hamlin sees blacks as full-fledged Americans, not as poor sisters demanding reparations. His fresh, progressive ideas will be embraced by most black voters, and Mr. Hamlin should have a bright future as our representative in Washington.'" Hamlin laughed, "They were right on the money."

"That's interesting," Spivey said. She did not agree, but there was nothing to be gained by saying so.

"I'll be a civil rights pioneer in a lot of ways. Black people have always opened things up for other groups who suffer discrimination. Just think, my wife would be the first Native American First Lady!" He forced a laugh, thinking that Spivey might not be aware of his wife back in Idaho. But, in fact, she knew almost everything about him. She had read all the research before she met him.

"What do you really think of the bill in the House?" Spivey asked, changing the subject as the car moved through the darkened park's winding roadway. She cuddled closer to him and squeezed his arm.

"We'll talk that over. There are a lot of ins and outs," he said as he leaned down and kissed her earlobe. Hamlin was avoiding the question because he had actually intended to press for nearly all the changes in the diamond bill that Spivey had suggested before he met her. Now his mind was on other matters. He let his hand slip back down to her knee.

"What's your long-range strategy?" she asked, undistracted by his caresses.

"There's plenty of time to talk about that," he said.

"Oh, wait! My place is just up ahead. Slow down."

When she pointed to a townhouse, Hamlin turned off the headlights and stopped the car about twenty yards away.

"Look, why don't you get out here and walk the rest of the way," he said nervously. "With my marital situation and all, I don't think it's wise that we go in together—too many politicians caught with their keys in the wrong locks lately."

"You're a cautious one, aren't you? Okay, I'll wait for you inside."

"Give me ten minutes," he said.

Hamlin watched as Spivey left the car and walked to the door. When she was safely inside, he moved back about ten more yards so that the car was partially concealed by the foliage of an overhanging tree. He looked at his Rolex, then began tapping his fingers on the steering wheel, anticipating a night of delightful discoveries.

He didn't notice the Ford Expedition, which had stopped some ten yards behind him, because its occupants had also turned off the headlights. Although he was surprised, he wasn't shocked when an attractive young woman with a distressed look on her face tapped on his window. It was only after rolling down the window that he realized she was the same gorgeous creature who had been sitting at the bar in

Georgia Brown's with the man in the jogging suit. By then it was too late. Before he could react, the barrel of a revolver slammed against his forehead.

Christine Spivey sat on the sectional divan in her living room, sipping a glass of Taittinger Grand Cru Brut 1998. She had quickly changed into a slinky silk nightgown and dimmed the lights when she came inside. Now the voice of Luther Vandross crooned softly from her sound system. There was still more information that she wanted to get from Hamlin, and this, she thought, was the perfect setting to open him up—not only about his vote on the diamond legislation but also about how he, a freshman congressman, had risen so quickly. After what she thought must have been ten minutes, she stared at the antique clock on the mantle and realized it had been twelve minutes. She walked to the window, pulled the curtains aside, and looked out. Hamlin's Lexus was nowhere in sight. Assuming he had driven around the block, she sat back down and lit a cigarette. Five minutes later, she went to the window and looked again. There was still no sign of Hamlin or his car. She pulled a raincoat over her nightgown and walked to the curb but still didn't see the car.

Exasperated, she returned to the couch. This didn't make sense. He had been eager and raring to go. For the next twenty minutes, Spivey kept returning to the window expecting to see Hamlin's blue Lexus out front. Finally, after more than a half hour, she turned off the music and lights, and angrily stomped up to her bedroom. That son of a bitch, she thought. Nobody stands me up. Lying in bed, she consoled herself by planning revenge on Hamlin in the future. Her real worry was how she would explain this to her boss the next day.

That problem was solved at 7:15 A.M. the next day when she turned on the *Today Show* and heard Katie Couric interviewing one of the congressman's colleagues. Dave "Tater" Hamlin had been killed when his car went out of control and plunged into Rock Creek. He had not been wearing a seat belt and apparently had been drinking heavily.

"This is a grave loss for the Congress and the country," Representative John Durham intoned. "The entire nation is in mourning."

Washington was shocked.

Christine Spivey gasped and nearly spilled a brimming cup of hot coffee onto her lap before grabbing the remote and switching to CNN.

SIX

Renee Rothchild sat at the desk in her study and stared at the obituary page of *Le Monde* in disbelief. Although the headline was written in French, she read it without a problem. She had lived in Paris for the past twenty years and considered herself European; as well as her native English, she spoke fluent French, Italian, German, and Spanish.

But on this day, as she read the paper, she wished that she had never learned to read French at all. She wished that she had never stepped off the airplane into the balmy Parisian air and a new life twenty years ago. If she hadn't, she would never have met Lester Bennett, the sax player from her hometown in Louisiana who'd been, without a doubt, the love of her life. She wouldn't be reading about his death, wedged between the weather report and a feature on the dedication of a new statue near the rue Vicomte.

Renee scanned the article four times, and still it didn't make sense. Lester Bennett, the renowned jazz musician, had been discovered dead in his exclusive apartment house on the rue du Petit-Pont, an apparent suicide by hanging. An investigation was under way, although police inspectors found no evidence of foul play. Preliminary findings indicated that he was intoxicated and officials suspect that he was despondent over his stalled career. The body would be turned over to a representative of the family who was flying in from the United States. A host of small memorial services were being planned for later dates.

Lester was dead, and Renee couldn't avoid the thought that she was at least indirectly implicated in his passing. Klaus Svrenson had warned her that some problems had arisen, but neither she nor Lester thought it would come to this. She had allowed herself to get caught up in a whirlpool of deception and easy money, and, now, she couldn't see a way out.

For a moment, Renee let her mind drift back to the past—the long evening strolls she and Lester took along the Seine and how he used to play delicate notes on his sax as they sat in the perfumed garden of the magnificent basilica of St-Germain-le-Doré with its massive marble columns and golden mosaics. It was one of Lester's favorite places in the world because, more than 1,500 years ago, there was a temple dedicated to the goddess Isis located on that very spot. No matter where they traveled, Lester always brought Renee back to the gardens of the Doré because he said that Nubian goddesses should try to keep company together as often as possible.

They had loved each other through the best and worst of times. At one point, they were the most sought-after jazz artists in Paris. The contrast between her sensuous, velvety vocals and the airy pirouettes of Lester's soprano sax made their music seem like an ethereal dance that only the two of them could truly understand. Everyone else came along for the ride, hoping to move close enough to glimpse and feel the magic.

But then there were many, many dark days of drinking and screaming and accusations. Lester had even hit her once when he was high on drugs. But he never did it again because Renee picked up a telephone and bashed him on the head with it until he was unconscious. She rode with him in the ambulance, crying and begging him to wake up and be all right. When Lester did regain consciousness, he refused to press charges against her. His drug addiction had been revealed, however, and the scandal made headlines. In some tabloids, both of them were portrayed as drug users, even though Renee's friends knew that she had never even smoked a joint. Still, the pair couldn't go anywhere without photographers hounding them.

When Renee opened her jazz club, The Emerald Isle, on rue de Furstenberg in St-Germain-des-Prés, Lester was right there by her side. The exclusive club had initially been a resounding success. The opulent decor gave it a palatial feel, with marble inlays on the walls, crystal chandeliers, heavy red-velvet drapes, and a balcony on the mezzanine reserved for special celebrity or royal patrons. Tapered candles and delicate, crimson orchids adorned every table. An army of waiters in crisp, black tuxedos bustled back and forth, serving and pampering the guests. Some of the most well respected and influential musicians in the world had graced Renee's stage.

Despite its popularity and splendor, The Emerald Isle quickly and inexplicably began losing money a year after it opened. Lester, of course, was there to console a confused and depressed Renee.

It had taken her more than two years to discover that Lester was stealing from her. He'd been bankrupted by unscrupulous people with get-rich-quick scams, which he was suckered into on the promise of regaining the money he'd squandered on his drinking, drug, and gambling addictions. Renee cut him off at that point and refused to speak with him for five years.

Then, out of the blue, Lester showed up on her doorstep. He camped out there for three days straight, claiming that he had something important to say to her and he wouldn't leave until she agreed to hear him out. On the third day, Renee decided to listen from her balcony. Lester told Renee, and everyone else passing by on the rue Bonaparte, that he'd been addicted to heroin for more than six years. It had almost cost him his life but he hadn't been able to stop. Even after Renee ended it with him, the addiction had been too strong for him to do the right thing. For the last three years, he'd lived as a vagrant, reduced to sleeping in St-Julien-le-Pauvre Park, too ashamed of himself to contact anyone from his old life.

Then one day last winter, he had seen Renee, still the most stunning, regal woman he'd ever met, walking by him in St-Julien-le-Pauvre. He had waved to get her attention. But in his wretched, debilitated state, she hadn't even recognized him. That was when he knew he had to change. He'd been sober for six months when he appeared outside her apartment, and he asked if she would agree to at least have lunch with him. Nothing fancy—he was pretty broke—but he'd be honored if she said yes.

That was a year ago, and they had been drawing closer ever since. Renee had almost been able to see a future for them. The only thing that had troubled her was the fact that, about six months ago, Lester had suddenly come into a very large sum of money and he wouldn't tell her where he had gotten it. He just said that he was in the process of starting a new business. When Renee began pulling away from him, Lester finally disclosed the source of his newfound wealth. It was a grisly, lurid business, and she was shocked and uneasy. But when faced with the thought of being without Lester again, Renee decided that his fate was her fate. In for a penny, in for a pound.

Now Lester was dead. He'd hanged himself, the paper said. But she knew it wasn't true. Lester wouldn't have killed himself, not now. She saw him two days before his death, and they had planned a vacation in

Rome. And he hadn't drunk since they got back together. She was sure of it.

If they would do this to Lester, was she safe? Panic gripped her, and she dropped her head onto the desk and began to cry.

The sharp trill of the telephone brought her back to reality. Renee almost didn't answer it. She didn't want to deal with anyone right now. Not even friends offering well-meant condolences. But then she remembered that Paolo, her bodyguard, said he was going to call her to see if she needed him to escort her to the club that afternoon. Yes, she definitely needed him. Renee was afraid, but she couldn't stay away from the club. Not now, after what had just happened. No matter how badly she wanted to curl up into a ball and disappear, she couldn't just not show up. She wiped her eyes and her nose on the back of her hand and picked up the phone, expecting to hear Paolo's throaty, French accent on the other end of the line.

Instead she heard a woman's voice say: "Hello? Hello?"

"Who is this?" Renee demanded. "What do you want?"

"Ms. Rothchild? You don't know me, but my name is Mariana Blair. I'm a reporter from the *Glo*—"

Renee slammed the phone into the cradle. She put her head down on the desk and, once again, began to sob.

When the phone rang again, Renee snatched it up and screamed into the receiver: "Don't you people have any respect at all? *Mon dieu!* A man is dead and I suppose all that means to you is another quote for your bloody article. Well I have nothing to say. And if you call me again I will take action against—"

"Please, I don't mean to disturb you, madam, especially in such a time of grief, but I think you'll want at least to hear me out. It seems that the music world has suffered a string of untimely deaths, including a good friend of mine, Brixton Hewitt, and now your, uh, friend Lester Bennett. Who knows who could be next."

Mariana let her words hang in the air between them. She waited out the silence, feeling Renee Rothchild begin to panic on the other end of the line.

She's wondering exactly how much I know, Mariana thought. Well, let her wonder.

After an extremely long pause, Renee whispered, "Who are you? What do you want?"

"As I tried to say before, I'm a reporter from the *Globe* in London. I wanted to ask you a few questions, if I may?"

Renee remained silent, so Mariana continued, "I'm sure you're familiar with Edward 'Ruff Daddy' Shelton? As you may have heard, he was in the car with Brixton Hewitt when Brixton was killed. There's reason to suspect that Ruff Daddy may have been the intended target, not Brixton. Tell me, are you currently on speaking terms with Ruff Daddy? I ask you because I have it from a reliable source that he met Lester at the Lido the last time he was in Paris. You wouldn't happen to know anything about that, would you?"

"I have no idea what you're talking about."

"Really? That's too bad. So I guess you wouldn't happen to know Klaus Svrenson or his Dutch associate Kees Van derVall either?"

Renee was dumbfounded. Rage, fear, curiosity, indignation, and grief welled up in her so strongly that she could barely speak. Who was this woman? How did she know about any of this? In the end, Renee's rage and fear got the best of her.

"How dare you question me? How dare you call me, especially at a time like this, to ask these ridiculous questions? It's cruel and insensitive and just sick. You should be ashamed."

"Please, Ms. Rothchild, I didn't mean to upset you any more than you already are. It's just that you must know how important the answers to these questions are right now. I believe that you, of all people, would want to take special care—"

"What? What did you just say? Was that a threat?"

"No, Ms. Rothchild. I'm not trying to threaten you in any way."

"That's right. You're not threatening me. You're just trying to play me for the fool and get me to spill my guts to you so you can turn around and run with any little scrap I can give you." Renee's voice turned husky and menacing.

Suddenly, she was no longer Renee Rothchild, international jazz diva. She became, once again, the young and hungry Edna Louise Byrd from the bayous of Louisiana—the Edna Louise Byrd who had scratched and clawed her way to the summit of the jazz world and refused to allow anyone to remove her from her perch.

"I told you once, I have nothing to say to you. I don't know the answers to any of your questions. I've never heard of this Van derVall or Klaus Svrenson. I'm giving you fair warning. If you call me again, even once, you'll regret it. I promise."

Renee slammed the phone down and began pacing her office like a caged animal. Thoughts of Lester and his dashed dreams and promises flooded her mind along with the realization that she too was now in danger. She had no idea how she was going to make it through the next hour, much less through the rest of the day or week.

She couldn't consider that now. She had to take this one day at a time. First, she had to contact Lester's family. Then she had to call Paolo. He would protect her. He would make sure that she got to the club and back home again in one piece, without losing her mind along the way.

Later, at The Emerald Isle, Renee had the unmistakable feeling that she was being observed. The feeling was so intense that she hesitated mingling with the guests as she normally did. Most nights, she was as much a source of entertainment as the famous musicians whom she booked to perform. But tonight she couldn't trust herself in that role. She avoided the patrons, speaking to no one but Paolo.

Paolo attributed her agitation to the fact that she hadn't had even a second to herself to grieve in private. He repeatedly told her just to go home, but when she said no, he assumed that she simply could not face her grief alone. So he stayed nearby, waiting outside her second-floor office. She remained in the office throughout the evening and, except for several phones calls that she had to make, spoke to no one.

At the end of the night, when Renee asked him to stay with her in her townhouse, he agreed. She'd looked terrified all night, poor thing. It was the least he could do. Renee and Paolo slipped out the back door of the club just after 1 A.M. and headed to her home.

The next morning, they left early to return to the club. Renee told Paolo she had to meet with some business associates.

They came out of Renee's townhouse and turned left onto rue Jacob and then right onto the small side street, rue de Furstenberg. It was a short walk from her home to the club, but that morning, Renee felt as though it would never end.

The scene outside was as quiet and picturesque as usual. The tall empress trees were in full bloom, with their large, mauve blossoms glowing in the morning light. The houses on either side of the street had been converted from stables and, unlike her own modern town-house a few blocks away, were centuries old, with low doorways and brick-and-stone facades. They lent just the right old-world charm that, to Renee, was the hallmark of good taste and beauty. But she barely noticed any of it that day. She was unable to focus. Her thoughts were on this afternoon's meeting with Lester's associates.

Renee sat behind her desk for two hours staring off into space before she heard a knock at the door. Slowly, she rose and walked over to the locked door. She opened both locks with the key that she wore around her wrist and swung the door open. It was Paolo.

"Your guests have arrived, ma'am. They're downstairs, waiting at a table."

"Good," Renee said. "I'll be right down."

When Renee came downstairs, her guests were seated at a table near the bandstand and Paolo was standing by the bar, some fifty feet away, where Renee had instructed him to stay. She knew that from that distance he couldn't hear what would be said but he would be able to watch and protect her if something went wrong.

Paolo watched as the visitors rose to greet Renee. The slim woman with long, auburn hair stood and hugged Renee, seemingly consoling her, and the wiry, dark-skinned man in the gray suit shook her hand before they sat down. At first, the man sat back in his chair, almost disinterestedly, as Renee and the woman leaned toward each other whispering. The woman kissed Renee's cheek as Renee dabbed tears from her eyes, then turned toward the man who glared at them impatiently. Paolo never took his eyes off of them.

At the table, the man cleared his throat and said, "I think it's time we got down to business."

"I suppose you're right," the woman said.

"So, Renee, have you arranged things here?" the man asked.

"Just so you both know, I don't feel right about this," Renee said, still dabbing at her eyes.

"I know, dear, I know. But it's what Lester would have wanted. You know that," the woman said.

Renee stared at the woman momentarily, then straightened in her chair and turned to the man. "Yes. I did. I made two or three calls yesterday after I got your call. The funeral home is about a kilometer from here. You'll be allowed to inspect the body. A man named Pierre Chadenet will be with you and he's going to step out of the room while you pay your last respects, and when he comes back into the room, he'll seal the coffin. The coffin cannot be reopened, not by customs or anyone else. Only you or Lester's sister, the sole surviving member of his family, can have the coffin opened when you arrive back in the States."

Renee handed the woman a key. She took it and placed it in her purse without a word.

"Is there anything I can do for you?" she asked.

Renee shook her head. "I just want this to be over with. I don't think I can continue. None of it was my idea. Lester would never have purposely put me in danger, and now that he's gone I want out. I think I'm going to leave Paris for a while—after I hear from you and I know that you've arrived safely in the States."

"Don't worry," the woman said. "We're leaving this afternoon no later than four P.M. I'll be sure to call you the minute we land so that you know everything went all right. In fact, I'll call you from the plane so that you know we boarded with no problems. You deserve to take as much time for yourself as you need."

"That's what I intend to do," Renee said, wiping her eyes.

"Still, I'd think about your decision to quit if I were you. It may not be as easy as you think, dear," the woman said, as she and her companion stood up.

Renee stared at them silently, as Paolo escorted them out of the club. When he closed the door and returned, Renee started up the stairs to her office. "I have a lot of work to do, Paolo," she said, "and I don't think I can face the crowd when we open. Can you take care of things down here tonight?"

Paolo nodded.

Renee remained in her office all afternoon. She sat at her desk, going over the books, ordering liquor, wine, food, and other supplies, and making phone calls. She had resolved to leave Paris for at least a month or two. She would pack tomorrow and get a flight to New Orleans the following day. No one but Paolo would know where she was going. But she couldn't even think about leaving unless she left everything in perfect order for Jean, the club's general manager. He was a hard worker and extremely loyal, but not the sharpest person in the world when it came to making decisions. So if Renee really planned to escape in two days, it meant that she had a long, hard night's work ahead of her.

Around eight o'clock, the club began filling up. She could feel the excitement and the energy in the crowd. The Junior Mance Trio would be playing later, and she expected a big turnout. At any other time, the laughter and joy would be intoxicating to her. But on this night, the sound of the slow, sensuous jazz piano solo, which was being piped into the room, and the appreciative murmurs of the crowd made her heart ache.

No one was watching her. No one but Paolo and Jean even knew that she was in the club that night. She hadn't left her second-floor office since she went down to the kitchen around five o'clock and brought up a thermos filled with frothy cappuccino. The kitchen staff hadn't even begun to arrive at that point. No outsider could have gotten into the club. Still, as much as she berated herself for being frightened and panicky, Renee made sure to lock both locks on her office door and shut the window.

Around two in the morning, the crowd downstairs began to thin and soon the noise, laughter, and music faded out. Renee heard the sound of Paolo shutting and locking the front doors. About a half hour later, she heard the opening and closing of the heavy metal door in the back as the kitchen help packed up and left for the night. As was customary, the front doors opened and shut a few minutes later. Paolo had let Jean out, she thought. Afterward, The Emerald Isle was silent.

Too silent.

Renee waited for Paolo to come trudging up the stairs, weary after a long night, and help her put away the evening's receipts. But she didn't hear the usual tinkle of glasses, which signaled that he was preparing his special cosmopolitans. Nor did she hear the whir of the espresso machine, indicating that he was making cappuccinos instead.

Nothing.

Then Renee heard a muffled, creaking sound as someone ascended the wooden stairs. She assumed it was Paolo until she realized that the footsteps were much too light. Paolo was over six feet tall and weighed

240 pounds; it was definitely not his heavy, forceful gait. Nor was it Jean, since he had apparently left. And if it wasn't Paolo, who was it?

When someone pushed against the door and tried to turn the doorknob, she leapt up and backed away from the desk. Terrified and trembling, she eased her way over toward the telephone, which sat in its cradle on top of the filing cabinet. She picked up the phone and hurriedly dialed the police.

The key turning in the door lock froze her. That was impossible! No one, not even Paolo, had a key. She had the only one and it was still hanging from her wrist. Suddenly, complete panic gripped her, and she screamed as loudly as she could: *"Paolo! Paolo! Help me!"*

A second later, a hand muffled her scream and another gripped her throat. She dropped the phone, and, just before the intruder ripped the cord from the wall, a hysterical voice could be heard screaming at the other end of the line — *"Qui est-ce? Qui êtes-vous?"*

New York

Perspiring lightly, Kim Carlyle flopped down on her couch with a towel around her neck; she was still wearing her powder-blue jogging shorts and a tank top. It was after 11 A.M., and she had just finished her morning run in the park and was ready to settle into the daily routine of unwinding with coffee, yogurt, and the daily papers before she showered and left for her office. The message button on her telephone answering machine was blinking, but, after checking the caller I.D. and seeing that it was from Rick Dupre, she ignored it. She had picked up the late edition of the *New York Daily News*, and, when she opened it, she was stopped by one of the first headlines she saw:

JAZZ GREAT SUCCUMBS
TO HEROIN OVERDOSE IN PARIS

Below it, there was a picture of a young and vibrant Renee Rothchild poised elegantly in front of a microphone, beaming with confidence at her audience.

Renee Rothchild, born Edna Louise Byrd, in Westwego,
Louisiana, in 1948, was found dead of an apparent overdose by
her bodyguard at approximately 2:30 A.M. at The Emerald Isle,
the nightclub she owned in Paris. Drug paraphernalia was found
in her office. Police sources say they are attempting to determine
whether or not there had been any foul play. They are question-
ing the bodyguard, the general manager of the club, and the
staff. The bodyguard claimed that he had been in the basement
completing the liquor inventory. He heard nothing unusual, but
when he came upstairs to check on Renee, her office door was
open and she was dead.

The article was brief, since, from what Kim could make out, the incident had happened the night before.

It went on to say that the police inspector in charge of investigating Ms. Rothchild's death noted that a few bruises had been found on her wrists, which may have been the result a struggle or Ms. Rothchild may have been restrained. Mention was made of the fact that Renee Rothchild's longtime companion, Lester Bennett, had also recently committed suicide in his Paris apartment. Authorities were going to continue investigating both cases vigorously.

The story intrigued Kim. She didn't know Lester Bennett personally, but she had been introduced to Renee Rothchild when she visited Paris a year or so before. She had always admired Renee's music, and when they met she had been impressed with her elegance and charm.

Their deaths reminded her of Tiffany. And that in turn led her to think about the drive-by killing of Brixton from which Ruff Daddy narrowly escaped. Suddenly, it seemed that the black music industry was under siege. Tiffany, Brixton, and now Renee and Lester Bennett. There was no apparent connection, and, given the rivalries and hostilities in the world of hip-hop, the Brixton drive-by was not that unusual. Still, the coincidence of all these deaths in a week or so seemed strange. And Kim had been trained never to accept coincidence as a satisfactory explanation for anything. When she started with the NYPD, Lt. Jackson had told her, "If it crawls like a snake and hisses like a snake, look out for the venom."

When she left her apartment she decided that on Sunday, after returning from her Los Angeles trip, she would call her old friend, Lt. Jackson, and arrange to have a drink with him. At least she could air her thoughts and get a reaction from a pro. Perhaps he had some conclusive information on Tiffany Jones's death. If she knew Tiffany had really died of a diabetic seizure, as everyone assumed, it might help her get rid of all these nagging suspicions.

SEVEN

Los Angeles — Saturday, July 28

Kim Carlyle guided the rented convertible, a silver-gray Mercedes, to a halt at the corner of Sunset Boulevard and La Cienega. She had met two senior Warner Records executives at the Polo Lounge in the Beverly Hills Hotel earlier in the afternoon and, if her instincts were correct, the multirecord deal for saxophonist Charlie Holt and his fusion-jazz group had been sealed. After returning to her suite at the Chateau Marmont, she had discarded the severe, power business-suit worn for the meeting and rested for a few hours before changing into the slinky Chanel pantsuit that she now wore. Tonight's festivities called for something more chic and relaxed.

She glanced quickly at the visor mirror to assure herself that the wind and heat weren't destroying her hairdo, then pulled away, heading west toward the Pacific Coast Highway. The bash for Cheeno— the rapper turned actor who had recently gotten rave notices and upturned thumbs from critics across the country for his performance in the film *Crack Baby*—was due to kick off at nine. The sun was just beginning its descent toward a typically hazy L.A. horizon, and she figured she had about an hour to get to Cheeno's newly acquired digs in Malibu. Cheeno had suddenly become one of her hottest clients; she had to make an appearance, and she didn't want to be late.

It was twilight when she turned off the Pacific Coast Highway onto Winding Way, a narrow, snakelike road that led up into the hills overlooking the Pacific. The road was intersected by short lanes and cozy culs-de-sac with houses nestled close together near the bottom of the hill. But as she ascended the steep grade, the lots and houses ballooned in size and the small crossing lanes were replaced by wide circular driveways leading to sprawling mansions. Near the top, a huge banner had been stretched across the road:

CHEENO—IN THE HOUSE.

She smiled to herself as she turned into the wide driveway, wondering what the old residents thought of their irrepressible new neighbor. Cheeno had a knack for outrageous self-promotion, and understatement was definitely not his thing.

It was only 9:15, but all available parking in the drive had already been taken and a line of limousines and expensive cars stretched almost to the road. A half-dozen young male attendants, attired in glistening black gaucho pants and scant red vests opened to reveal their well-developed pecs, scurried around assisting guests from their limos and whisking unchauffered cars off to be parked. Kim couldn't resist thinking that every one of them looked as if he had just stepped out of Cheeno's latest music video.

Inside the grand, colonnaded, neocolonial mansion, the heavy beat of Cheeno's mega hit, "Booty Power," literally rocked the space. Kim was greeted by a group of hostesses clad in red vests—only slightly less revealing than those worn by the outside attendants—and skimpy thongs that boldly accentuated that part of the anatomy celebrated by the rapper's lyrics. One of the perky young mascots approached, literally bouncing over to Kim, and led her through the domed foyer into a massive living room. There guests gathered in small groups sipping champagne and attempting to talk over the music, which blared from concealed speakers. Cheeno's latest music video was being displayed on a huge flat-screen monitor suspended high on a wall near the rear of the room.

Arched entrances led, on her left, to an imposing dining room and, on her right, to a den or game room, which was stocked with electronic gadgets and games. The semicircular staircases on either side of the huge room ascended to a spacious balcony that served as entranceway to more than a half-dozen bedrooms but was now filled with candlelit tables. A few guests had already taken up positions there and sat gazing down at the mob below them. Through a wall-length expanse of sliding glass doors at the rear of the room was a tiled patio, and beyond that an Olympic-size pool sandwiched between two bubbling, oversize spas.

Kim accepted a glass of Dom Perignon from a smiling waiter who, in perfect time to Cheeno's music, acrobatically danced among the guests, balancing a dozen or so crystal goblets on a silver tray. She took a sip then stood to the side, sizing up the crowd. She immediately noted that scattered throughout the room were more than a dozen security guards; despite an attempt to blend in, their rigid postures, darting eyes, and dark, off-the-rack worsted suits stood out like neon signs. Cheeno had told her he was expecting more than one hundred guests, and it seemed that at least half of them had already arrived. Among them were some top executive suits, a few prominent stars, and celeb-status directors and producers. She had seen Debbie Allen, John Singleton, Clive Davis, Reuben Cannon, Tyra Banks, Quincy Jones, one of the Wayans clan, and either Russell Simmons or an exact look-alike—each holding court before a group of seemingly spell-bound listeners.

Rick Fox from the Lakers and, judging from his extreme height, another NBA player huddled with two or three friends whom Kim didn't recognize but assumed were pro football players because of their hulking physiques. They stood near the glass doors leading to the patio, laughing and alternately peering out over the rapidly growing crowd inside or out at the half-dozen female revelers frolicking in the pool in fantasy-inspiring bikinis. Then there was the younger Holly-wood set, the nouveau successful crowd that had broken through and soared to fame, fleeting or otherwise, on one or another of the sitcoms that flourished on the UPN, WB, and Fox networks. Still, this was not your typical Hollywood party.

Most guests were clearly from the *Source/MTV/Vibe* rap set—in town for the upcoming *Source* Awards, Kim concluded. There were some West Coast rappers, but most seemed to be part of Cheeno's posse, a group of friends, musicians, and acolytes whom the rap-cum-movie star had brought with him when he left Newark. The rappers were easily distinguished from the Armani- and Gucci-clad Hollywood types by their attire. They were decked out in an assortment of colorful jackets, vests, and jeans or baggy pants (one leg rolled up) inspired by designers ranging from No Limit, Tommy Hilfiger, John Varvatos, and Sean John to The Gap and Banana Republic. Nearly all wore some kind of headware—including caps, designer head-rags, outrageous fedoras, berets, and specialty hats like construction helmets and man-nequin caps. Most were bejeweled with enough ice or, as a *Sex and the City* character had called it, "ghetto gold" to stock a New York dia-mond district outlet. They were not difficult to spot. At first glance, Kim's favorite was the *Loose Ends* MC who wore old-fashioned clod-hoppers and cut-off, black-and-white pajama bottoms under an elegant antique tuxedo jacket with tails. Except for a few who had opted for the revealing, minimal outfits favored by Lil' Kim, their female counter-parts were less conspicuous.

This evening the sometimes explosive rivalry between the rap factions appeared to be under control. Although they clowned, trash-talked, and tried upstaging one another, no animosity was on display; a few of the East Coast Ain't No Thang crew had even joined Watts Up, a West Coast group, and were lifting their glasses in a toast in front of the TV monitor. The rappers' boisterous antics, along with the blaring video, set the upbeat, almost raucous tone of the party.

Kim smiled and calmly scanned the room, nodding to a few friends before setting out to mingle with the guests. She was long past being star-struck, unless, of course, business required she give that impression. As she often joked, she was a show-business agent by accident and a sleuth by nature; seeming oddities and the unusual captured her attention much more than celebrities. Still certain people had to be given their props; so when she started making the rounds, she rapped briefly with Singleton, injected herself into a conversation between Quincy and Debbie Allen, and briefly cornered a Fox executive who had called about one of her clients. Before long, however, she gravitated toward a group of intriguing peripheral characters she had never met.

A tall, dark-skinned man wearing a Nehru jacket and tasseled fez, whose facial scarification suggested he was African, stood near the archway leading to the dining area talking to two bespectacled business types in Brooks Brothers suits. The two men, whose pale skin suggested a strong aversion to sunlight, gestured toward the wiry, nut-brown-complexioned black man with heavy dreadlocks, dark rimless sunglasses, wool trousers, and a brightly colored polyester short-sleeve shirt who stood beside them. At a Malibu party, the quartet seemed odd or, at best, unusual. They were engaged in heated conversation but, when Kim approached, the talk ceased abruptly; the black man with dreads turned and quickly moved into the dining room.

"Didn't mean to break up the caucus," Kim laughed. "Just making the rounds. But I seemed to have disturbed your friend."

"Oh, not to worry," the younger Brooks Brothers suit replied in a clipped English accent, "he was never a very sociable chap. Perhaps, like the rest of us, he was simply overwhelmed by your beauty." He bent at the waist and, lifting Kim's hand, softly kissed it. "I'm Winthrop — Winthrop James," he said with a mischievous glint in his eye.

"I'm Kim Carlyle . . . from New York," she said, momentarily taken aback by the lingering, somewhat seductive kiss.

"Yes, I've heard of you — you are an artists' representative if I'm not mistaken. Formerly Tiffany Jones's agent. Am I correct?"

Kim nodded, surprised that he knew of her.

"This is Jonathan Wims, a business associate," he said, nodding toward the other suit, "and Paul Mawuli, a visitor from Liberia."

"And what brings you to Hollywood?" she asked.

"Oh, just boring business transactions," Winthrop said. "Contracts, inventories, debits, and such — nothing that would interest you show-business movers and shakers."

"And you, Mr. Mawuli?" Kim asked, smiling up at the tall African.

"Winthrop and I attended Oxford together," Mawuli said; "we met, purely by chance, in the bar at the Park Hyatt in Century City. It was I who suggested he accompany me to Mr. Cheeno's, ah, what is the idiom . . . blow-out." He laughed ingenuously. "And, as usual, I'm impressed with the . . . ardor of your festivities."

"Well, we do what we can," Kim laughed, "but I should admit that this bash is hardly representative of our . . . *festivities*. Anyway, you've traveled a long distance. I assume it was not just to honor Cheeno."

"You are an inquisitive beauty, aren't you?" Mawuli said, smiling. "No, not exactly. In fact, my secretary had been instructed to call you in New York. You see, I am here to propose that Mr. Cheeno consider shooting his next film in Liberia. Financially, it could be a windfall for him since costs are minimal — no annoying problems with unions, you understand. And, my group, well, we're interested in expanding our investments—"

"Paul, you always go on so," Winthrop interrupted, forcefully grabbing Paul's arm. "I'm certain that Ms. Carlyle hasn't the slightest interest in the details of your organization. After all, this is a party. Why don't we get another drink and get into the spirit of things."

"On the contrary," Kim said, "it's a fascinating proposal and I'd—"

"Well, perhaps the two of you can talk about it later. For now, I think we should mingle, take in some of this wonderful ambience," Winthrop said, as he led his companions away.

They had disappeared into the crowd before Kim could object.

Kim considered following them, then decided she'd ask Cheeno about the mysterious trio. She accepted another glass of champagne from a dancing waiter and made her way to the patio. A few of the rappers had disrobed and joined the group of would-be starlets and dancers who cavorted half nude in the pool or lounged in the Jacuzzi. An attendant approached Kim as she stood watching them.

"If you'd like to swim, ma'am, you may change in the cabana," she said, pointing to the wooden bathhouse at the top of the stairs near the Jacuzzi to the left of the pool. "There are swimsuits or, if you prefer, no suit is necessary."

"No, thank you," Kim said. "I don't *prefer.*"

As she returned to the living room, the lights blinked several times, then dimmed before a spotlight focused on the balcony above the crowd. A minute later, Cheeno stepped out of one of the rooms, lifted his arms above his head, then dramatically bowed as his posse led a salvo of yelps and screams. At five-ten and 165 pounds, his slight frame was dwarfed by the two enormous bodyguards who stood behind him. They scowled menacingly as they surveyed the dim room, and followed him down the stairs staying just outside the circle of flickering light that traced his descent.

The pandemonium, orchestrated mostly by Cheeno's own posse,

continued for a least five minutes after the star reached the bottom of the
stairs. Dressed in Prada clogs and a loose-fitting beige linen shirt-suit by
Sean John, which was set off by a diamond-studded sterling silver
pendant spelling out his name, he basked in the applause—preening,
grinning, and mimicking a few dance steps from his "Booty Power"
video, which was still playing on the monitor. Finally, the lights went up
again to a chorus of, "Cheeno . . . Cheeno in the house! Cheeno . . .
Cheeno in the house!"

Kim smiled, half amused and half admiring. She was still amazed at
some of the excess and bombast of her younger clients, but, at the
same time, she knew their youthful zeal and exaggerated style was
what got them over. And when they got over, she also profited. Most
certainly, twenty-three-year-old Cheeno was getting over.

It was he who, a year and a half before, had led her to the producer
who backed his first film, which he had written. And, even when he
signed with her three years ago, before cutting his first single, he
seemed to be prospering. Most of her young clients struggled before
they made it, taking part-time service jobs and living in run-down studios or cheap hotels. Cheeno had left Newark and lived in a one-
bedroom Manhattan apartment when he came to her. He never talked
about his lifestyle—the apartment, car, or occasional trip to Europe—
except to say that he had a mentor; and she never asked any further
questions. Frankly, she didn't want to know. He seemed like a good
enough kid, and she was happy for him.

For nearly an hour after he appeared, Cheeno, shadowed by his
bodyguards, moved through the crowd greeting his guests. Finally, he
approached Kim.

"Hey, mama," he yelled, and lifted her in a bear hug.

"Told you I'd make it," she said. Cheeno was smiling broadly, but
as he talked to her his eyes kept darting around the room.

"Yeah. The party's live, ain't it!" he said.

"You outdid yourself, sugar," she laughed.

"It's only the beginning—only the beginning," he gushed. "I got plans I ain't even laid on you yet. Believe it, mama, I'm gon be big as Snoop, big as Tupac . . . bigger. You met Mawuli, right?"

"Yes, I did. So tell me, what's that about?"

"Not now, mama, we'll talk business tomorrow. You seen the crib, the pool, the Jacuzzis. This place is off the hook, ain't it? C'mon, let's go lay back and chill."

"No, sugar, I think I'll pass on that, but you go ahead."

Cheeno quickly scanned the room again, then turned and started for the patio with his bodyguards close on his tail. When he stepped outside, he turned to them. "Check it—I know you brothas got my back but I got to have a sec by myself. We got security out at the bath-house, ain't we?"

"No doubt," the taller, bald-headed guard snarled.

"A'ight. Y'all stay here. I'm gon change and go take a dip with these honeys. I paid for 'em, let's see what they about. Stay here and keep an eye out."

When Cheeno started toward the bathhouse, the guards stepped out-side the glass doors, watching his every move. Kim turned and headed toward the dining room. Time to try some of those hors d'oeuvres, she thought.

Just as she stepped into the dining room, Kim heard shouting from near the monitor where a group of rappers were watching a new video by Nelly. She turned and saw that a scuffle had broken out. Four or five guys were in each other's face and the scene was escalating. The volume of the cursing accelerated and, as nearby guests scurried to move back, a half-dozen security guards raced over and began pulling the men away from each other. It was then that the lights began flick-ering. At first Kim thought it was another staged happening, and, see-ing that the fight was under control, she ignored it and moved toward one of the buffet tables. Then, suddenly, the room went black—ink black. She pushed her way back toward the arched entrance, but absolutely nothing was visible. Unlike before, even the outside flood-lights illuminating the pool area were off.

"What the fucks goin' on?" someone shouted.

"Cheeno, turn on the damn lights. This shit ain't funny," another voice screamed.

"Nigga, get your hands off my ass!" a woman yelled and for a moment or two the sound of laughter rippled through the crowd.

Kim stood still initially, trusting that the problem would quickly be solved. But after five minutes, she began pushing her way through the pitch darkness toward what she thought was the patio. At least, she thought, outside there would be fewer people. By now a few people had begun igniting their lighters or striking matches to get some momentary illumination and, when someone held up a match near the patio, Kim spied the glass doors. She was almost there when the lights began flickering then snapped back on.

A moment later, someone outside screamed. Immediately she felt a surge of bodies pressing against her back. She was pushed out onto the patio. Another scream came from the Jacuzzi near the bathhouse, and Kim forced her way toward the sound and the crowd surrounding the Jacuzzi. Before she got there, one of the nude starlets fought through the mob yelling hysterically, "He's dead! Cheeno's dead!"

When Kim got to the edge of the Jacuzzi, Cheeno was lying face-up, floating in the gurgling water. She watched, horror-struck, as one of his bodyguards waded into the spa and dragged the rapper's lifeless body to the edge.

Kim sat on the corner stool near the rear of Dan Tana's in West Holly-wood and stared bleary-eyed at her third apple martini. It was her favorite L.A. bar now that Georgia's had closed, one of the few places in the city where she knew she'd find a true New York City flavor. The owner was a transplanted New York Italian, and he was intent on main-taining the Big Apple ambience. It didn't hurt that it was also relatively

close to the Marmont where she always stayed, and that she had
known the bartender, Frankie, when he worked in Sardi's in New York
before he fell in love with L.A.'s sun and surf. He always made sure
that a car was available to take her back to the hotel.

She had ordered the scampi, a specialty of the Italian chef, but she
had pushed it aside, unable to eat. She was still in shock. The drinks at
least blurred her mind and helped ease the pain.

It had been a circus when the police arrived at the Malibu mansion. With so many celebrities present, they weren't quite sure how to
handle the situation. And, of course, since a rapper had died, they
immediately assumed that it was some kind of hip-hop vendetta. They
had briefly questioned recognizable celebrities first, then allowed
them to go. Most of the others, including Kim, had also been interro-
gated only cursorily. Only the rappers had been grilled intensively
about their whereabouts during the ten minutes or so when the lights
were out. Few people had a real alibi because few saw anyone else during that time. The only light had come from matches and lighters.
Some insisted that they saw this or that person in the flickering light of
a nearby match or, if they were holding the flame, that they saw this or
that person standing near them. Kim wasn't convinced. She had stood
next to someone holding a lighter and, because it was held above their
heads, she couldn't with certainty say who it was.

The security guards had also told detectives that some of the guests
who had limo drivers waiting had left immediately after the body was
found. Security had tried to detain them, but this was Hollywood—no
celebrity wanted to be involved in a potential scandal. Some were
forced to stay because the valet parking attendants were told not to get
anyone's car. They followed instructions, unless, of course, they were
offered enough money to ignore them. So, under the circumstances,
any real investigation would have been compromised from the beginning.

Before she was questioned, Kim was able to get an idea of the story that was emerging by talking to some of the other guests. The bodyguards who had been watching Cheeno had apparently turned toward the crowd inside when the scuffle broke out among the rappers. It was then that the lights went out. When they turned to look for Cheeno, they couldn't see a thing. They had groped their way out to the pool area and one had even found the stairs leading to the bathhouse and gone up to search it. But he had not heard or seen anything. No one had.

When the lights went back on, it was one of the frolicking starlets who discovered the body. It appeared to be an accident, since, as one member of Cheeno's posse pointed out, the rap star couldn't swim. He must have stumbled and fallen into the Jacuzzi in the dark. If he had been slightly dazed, the story went, he could have easily drowned.

It wasn't an implausible theory, but Kim didn't buy it. The sequence of events seemed too well orchestrated. First the fracas near the monitor, which got the attention of both the security guards and Cheeno's bodyguards, and then the lights going out at precisely the right moment. It seemed too pat—*too* coincidental.

After being questioned, Kim expressed her reservations to Sergeant Furston, the chief investigator, but he dismissed her reasoning as fanciful speculation. When she argued that there was no reason for the lights to go out, he contended that it was probably the theatrical tinkering with the lighting during Cheeno's entrance or, maybe, the loudspeakers blasting out all that nonsensical hip-hop music that had caused the short. One of the sound men who worked with Cheeno, he explained, had gone into the kitchen and replaced a fuse. That's how the lights were turned on again.

"No, Ms. Carlyle," he said finally, "it was an accident, sure as I'm standing here. You know that boy couldn't swim, right."

Kim bristled at the word "boy," and struggled to maintain her composure.

Noticing her reaction, Sgt. Furston added, "Look, I'll consider what you've said, and we'll investigate further. But I'll bet you a Frank Sinatra CD that there was no foul play."

When Kim left the room, she was furious. And now, as she sipped her martini and stared at the list of musicians who had died, she still was. There was no apparent connection between the deaths of Tiffany, Brixton, Lester, Renee, and Cheeno, but she was certain that one existed.

"Frankie," she said, "would you call a car for me?"

"Right away, Kim," he said, "and I'm terribly sorry about your friends. Hang in there—don't let it get you down."

By the time she got back to the Marmont, Kim had decided that she would get to the bottom of this, no matter what it took. Something sinister was going on; she knew it now. Lying in bed that night, she made a note to call Maurice Jackson the next morning before leaving for the airport and confirm their meeting for the following day. Everything else could wait, she had to see him immediately.

EIGHT

LONDON—MONDAY, JULY 30

Alone in bed in her small London flat, Mariana Blair awoke in a cold sweat. She had been hounded by nightmares since Brixton's murder in Atlanta. She couldn't shake the thought that somehow she was responsible for his death. After all, she was the one who introduced him to Ruff Daddy and suggested that he go to America. Now she was worried about her own safety. This morning, she couldn't bring herself to get out of bed and report to work at the *Globe*. She had gone to her office infrequently since Brixton's death. Instead she stared blankly at the huge water spot on the ceiling above the bed. Outside, the roar of Kensington traffic signaled that the workday had begun, and, despite her anxiety, she knew that soon she would have to rise and get on with it.

Now, more than ever, she was deeply concerned about the story that had obsessed her for months. She felt guilty about it, but Brixton's death was more than just a personal loss. He and Kees Van derVall, the Dutch mobster whose activities had led her to stumble onto the story, were both dead. Authorities had not yet connected the deaths, and, although she couldn't prove there was a connection, she was certain that it wasn't mere coincidence.

Brixton had been with Ruff Daddy's entourage when he was killed, and she suspected that his death had been a mistake. She was certain that Ruff Daddy and Van derVall, along with Tiffany Jones's husband, Klaus Svrenson, had been involved in the conspiracy. They had been key, the only proven links she had discovered between the entertainers she *thought* were involved and the businessmen and criminals she strongly suspected were behind a multimillion-dollar diamond scam. Now Van derVall was dead and the other two had disappeared. Svrenson had dropped out of sight after Tiffany's death and neither she nor, as far as she knew, anyone else had heard from Ruff Daddy since the night of the shooting.

For the twenty-eight-year-old journalist, it was the biggest story of her young career—one that would lift her out of the anonymity of her entertainment beat assignment for the *Globe* and establish her reputation as an investigative reporter. Still, she wondered if she wasn't in over her head—if she shouldn't have gone to the police or shared the information she had uncovered with someone else at the paper. But she had never trusted her editor, Bill Wittington. She wasn't sure he would believe her if she confided in him, and, if he did, she feared that he would snatch the story away from her and reassign it to one of the older, more experienced reporters. She knew he wouldn't encourage her efforts.

No, shortly after meeting Kees Van derVall—six months ago when she was sent to Amsterdam to cover the rap concert at the Melkweg and Ruff Daddy had introduced him as the "importer"—Mariana decided that this would be her story, her ticket to fame. Even if she had to go it alone. Her suspicions had been aroused almost immediately because, among her journalist associates, Van derVall had a reputation as a small-time, but ambitious hood. Why, she wondered, was he so cozy with Ruff Daddy, a rap artist whom she had met shortly after taking the job at the *Globe*.

After the concert, when she returned to London, she did some snooping and found that Van derVall was not as small-time as others thought. Textel International Corporation, a supposed legitimate import/export business, was apparently a front. She had quickly discovered that local authorities were already investigating his possible involvement in a drug and arms smuggling ring. And by using her own contacts and even following Kees when he came to London, she uncovered much more. She was now convinced that he had connections ranging from African mercenaries and U.S. mobsters to high-level De Beers executives in London and shady diamond dealers in Antwerp. So, despite the danger, she wasn't ready to lay her cards on the table, not just yet. She had much higher aspirations.

For her the entertainment beat at the *Globe* was just a stepping stone. With the help of her father, a journalism professor, she had taken the job to get her foot in the door. It didn't matter that it was a tabloid, one of those sleazy half-size newspapers with screaming red headlines and lurid photographs that usually covered the entire front page. Nor did she care that its stories were often no more than unfounded gossip written to justify publication of some scandalous photograph, or that Britain's journalism establishment considered it utterly tasteless. She had been hired to cover celebrities and entertainers, to dig up as much dirt as she could on pop stars from Britain and elsewhere. And, except for one or two stories that unexpectedly turned out to have some real substance, for more than a year she had delivered just what they wanted. This story was different, however; she had stumbled onto a reporter's mother lode. It might well lead to a European Union Press Club Award and, if she was lucky, a best-selling book.

The story had dominated her life, and, two months ago, when she met Brixton at a Chelsea pub, it was the primary reason that she hadn't gotten closer to him. At first she was wary of the name he had taken — Brixton was the depressed district in south London that had been transformed into a battlefield in 1981. Rioting had broken out after authorities started Operation Swamp in response to a steep rise in street crime. Police officers began stopping and searching large numbers of black youths on Brixton's turf, and both white and black gangs had taken to the street. The young rapper had assumed the name as a symbol of pride in his community, and Mariana had initially thought he was some kind of militant black racist. When she got to know him, all that changed.

Yes, he was a tall, rugged, dark-brown man who exuded virility and race pride. But with his bedroom eyes and glistening smile, he reminded her more of the sexy American soul singer Teddy Pendergrass than of a militant agitator. And he attracted women nearly as readily as Teddy had, wealthy Hyde Park inhabitants as well as rebellious young groupies from the working-class districts. But there was no time for romance or even casual dalliance in her life, and she knew it. She resisted his advances and, although he wasn't accustomed to being put off by any woman, they managed to become good friends.

She not only loved being in the company of this brash, handsome, fast-rising star, but he was also a huge asset to making contacts in the entertainer world, particularly among blacks. It was mutually beneficial, since Brixton needed publicity and she made sure his name regularly popped up in *Globe* stories. Still, whenever he whispered that she would always be his "little rosy Brit sugar plum" and patted her bum, as he did quite often, she had difficulty resisting the impulse to invite him back to her flat.

Then, a few weeks after they met, Brixton asked her to introduce him to Ruff Daddy. At first, she resisted, using every excuse except the real one — her belief that Ruff Daddy was up to his neck in some sinister smuggling plot. When Brixton persisted, she finally gave in and called New York. Ruff Daddy met Mariana and Brixton at a pub in Mayfair on his next trip to London. The two men seemed to hit it off, and Ruff Daddy agreed to listen to some of Brixton's demos if he sent them back to the States. In the weeks before Brixton went to Atlanta, Mariana knew that the men talked several times, and, frankly, she began to worry that Brixton might be getting too close to Ruff Daddy. She even considered revealing her suspicions about the hip-hop entrepreneur. She never did. Now she realized it was one of the biggest mistakes of her life.

That's why, on the past two nights, she had returned to The Lollie, a seedy, overpriced dance club in Camden Town. She had prowled the trendy club looking for the mysterious little man whom Brixton had encountered there a couple of weeks before he went to Atlanta.

She remembered exactly what the man looked like—slender, red-haired with a pockmarked red face and pointed ears, like Mr. Spock. He had been dressed in dark slacks and a Savile Row sweater that stood out from the outrageous attire that even middle-class Londoners wore when visiting The Lollie. She was certain that he was somehow involved in Brixton's death.

"Get away from me, bloke!" Brixton had screamed when the man approached them on the dance floor. "This ain't no time for that shit!"

The man had continued toward them, pushing his way through the hoard of sweating, gyrating bodies. "I have to talk with you, mate," he insisted. "I know this is unexpected, but something has come up. . . ." He was shouting, but she and Brixton could barely hear his voice beneath the pounding reggae beat and the voice of Jamaican singer Marcia Hall chiming out the words to "I Shot the Sheriff."

At first, Mariana had thought he was just an extremely aggressive homosexual. Gays were an accepted part of the scene. The club was full of all kinds of Londoners who liked to mix with West Indians and Africans. But some older, more aggressive gays occasionally got out of hand; Brixton had been approached before. She had moved closer to her friend, ready to grab him in case he tried to punch the guy. When the man reached them and began talking to Brixton, however, she realized that they knew each other.

"You want to put something else in the mix?" he shouted. "That's whack—niggas ain't trippin' that way now."

"This is exactly the right time; no one can go to the police. Just listen to me—" the man said before staring at Mariana and cutting off the sentence. He grabbed Brixton's shirt, pleading, and finally Brixton accompanied him to the edge of the dance floor. Mariana stretched to her full height, peering at them over the crowd as they halted several yards away engrossed in heated conversation.

"Why?" Brixton yelled over the noise of the music. Mariana had strained to hear but only caught snatches of conversation.

"Everything . . . falling apart," the man had shouted, his voice intermittently drowned out by the music. When Brixton and the other man noticed that Mariana was watching and trying to make out what they were saying, the man had pointed angrily at her and, if she read his lips correctly, said, "Who the hell is she?"

Brixton said something in response, and they spoke for a few more minutes before the man turned and angrily walked away.

"Who was that?" Mariana had asked when Brixton returned. She shouted because the near-deafening sound of "Who Let the Dogs Out!" was now blaring from the loudspeakers.

"Nothing! No one—a bloody pimple on the backside of society!" Brixton shouted. "Let's dance." He grabbed her arm and pulled her back toward the middle of the floor. Closing his eyes, he threw himself into the music. They were quickly engulfed by the swarm of sweating, arm-waving revelers.

Later that evening Mariana had tried to get some answers from Brixton. He refused to talk about it; he didn't say a word before he left for the U.S. And when he died, she realized that she'd not only lost a close friend, but part of her story had died with him.

With Renee Rothchild, Van derVall, and Brixton gone, her strongest leads were Ruff Daddy; Petris Nicholov, Kees's Amsterdam associate; Klaus Svrenson, the American financier; and Riccardo Napolini, an American mobster. In addition, there were Kees's shadowy associates in Antwerp and at De Beers's central selling office in London, the unknown Asian woman who seemed to be popping up all over the place, and the curious little man who had appeared at The Lollie. She had been using all of her resources to find out more about Ruff Daddy, Nicholov, Svrenson, and the De Beers execs.

So far, however, she had uncovered very little about the extremely cautious Nicholov, whose activities were shielded by a veil of propriety. She was pursuing leads on Ruff Daddy and Svrenson, despite their disappearance, but little had surfaced. An informant had discovered that one of the De Beers execs made frequent trips to the Antwerp diamond district, and Mariana had some other good leads, but still she hadn't been able to pin down their actual identities. The Asian woman was more elusive than a ghost; Mariana had discovered that over the past six months she or someone who matched her description had been seen in Amsterdam, London, Paris, and God knows where else. No one seemed to know who she was or exactly what she did. But over the last few days, she had been more successful in tracking down the little man from the dance club.

She had quickly confirmed that he was gay and that his name was Freesley, Marvin Freesley, by haunting the trendy clubs and asking questions. A few of the regulars at The Box on Monmouth Street and the Freedom Cafe/Bar on Wardour Street had recognized her description and given her the name. And, once she had the name, a bartender at Balans on Old Compton Street had supplied the other information.

"Oh, that squirrelly little bloke," he'd laughed. "Always sniffing around scrounging for a pickup—lots of cash, you know. Wormy sort, though, usually went back to his flat alone. They say he lives over in Mayfair; I think he's a diamond cutter or some such thing."

That was last night, and she had left her number with the Balans contact and a dozen or so waiters or bartenders in other clubs saying, "Please, give me a call if you see him again, it's very important." She knew that tonight she'd make the rounds again. Maybe she'd get lucky and run into him. Perhaps even follow him and find out something about where and how he lived. At least, she knew who he was and, more important, what he did. The pieces were beginning to fit.

Today, however, she had to go back to work. She had taken the last two days off and she knew her editor would be furious. But even that thought wasn't enough to immediately rouse her. She lay immobile for another half hour before dragging herself from bed and trudging toward the bathroom.

Twenty minutes later, she stood in front of the full-length mirror on the back of the bathroom door. The hasty preparations had left something to be desired. The dark slacks-suit she wore accentuated her slim figure, ivory complexion, and dark hair. But with little time to fuss over it, she had just pulled her hair back in a tight bun. And despite the rouge she applied to her cheeks, overall she had a stark, squinty, almost anorexic look. She had never been beautiful, but with the right hairdo and makeup she could be very attractive in a haughty, professional way. In fact, given the right lighting, she looked a bit like the actress from *Friends*, Courteney Cox. A few men, Brixton among them, had told her so. And on those occasions when she had let her hair down and slipped into a fashionable miniskirt, she was even sexy.

When she started with the *Globe*, she had occasionally explored that part of her personality, slipping over the line between reporter and groupie, and joining several of the rock bands she covered in late-night trysts at their hotels. She had been twenty-six then and nothing had been out of bounds. After spending four years at the University of Michigan then returning home to get her M.A. in journalism from the University of Sheffield, she had spent nearly two years traveling and partying in Europe and North Africa. She was hungry for life and new experiences and had enjoyed every minute of it, even those few times when she'd gotten herself into some sticky situations. It was her father, a professor at Sheffield, who stopped it by cutting off her allowance and demanding she get a job. Her first six months at the *Globe* were little more than an extension of that youthful spree. Daddy would have erupted had he known how much carousing his little girl had done during that time.

She had changed, however, and gotten more serious, even before she stumbled onto the intrigue involving Kees and Ruff Daddy. After a punk rock lead singer high on Ecstasy had literally thrown her out at 6 A.M. on a Sunday morning and invited a sixteen-year-old nymphet into his hotel room, she vowed to keep the entertainers and celebrities she wrote about at arm's length. It was another reason that she and Brixton had never slept together. Earlier, she might have leapt at the chance.

Resigned to the impossibility of covering up the stress of the last few days, Mariana took one last look at herself and went to her computer. As always before leaving for work, she checked the Internet for breaking news. Initially nothing stood out, and she scrolled quickly through a list of new Mideast violence, Parliament doings, Bush's new agenda, the missing U.S. congressional assistant, and the Euro's downward spiral. When she saw a brief note on the Yank rapper Cheeno, she stiffened. He had apparently drowned in Los Angeles the night before. She didn't know him personally, but she had seen him perform over a year ago in one of the small clubs near Piccadilly Circus. The article immediately brought back memories of Brixton's death, and, when she finished, her mind was racing. Another rap musician dead under suspicious circumstances, could there be a connection? How far did this go?

She read it again, questioning her own instincts — trying to convince herself that it was just coincidence. When she finished the second time, she still wasn't sure. But one fact stood out from the familiar litany of celebrities present, innuendoes about rap record moguls' involvement, and police vagary about their findings—it was a brief mention of Cheeno's agent, "Kim Carlyle, a former NYPD detective, who was present when the incident occurred." Mariana didn't know the woman, but the name seemed familiar.

She stood and paced the floor for a few minutes, trying to place the name—Kim Carlyle. Then, realizing that she would be over an hour late for work, she returned to the computer. She quickly transferred the notes she had entered the previous day onto a floppy disk, then dragged the file on her hard disk to the trash. Before leaving her apartment, she replaced the floppy master disk in an envelope and slid it into the folder she had taped to the underside of a drawer in the bedroom bureau. A few minutes later she stepped out into the misty morning air.

Before entering the tube, she stopped at the corner newsstand to pick up the *Daily Mirror*, one of her paper's chief rivals. A photo of Britney Spears, half naked in a tank top and cut-off jeans, was spread across the front page. As the train rumbled through the London underground, she scanned the rest of the paper. But her thoughts kept returning to Kim Carlyle, and she racked her brain trying to determine why.

It was not until she reached Vauxhall Station that she made the connection. Kim Carlyle had been Ruff Daddy's agent when she met him. She had also been the agent of the diva who had recently died at the Apollo Theater, Tiffany Jones. She didn't know quite what to make of it, but as she dodged the Vauxhall Cross traffic and set out on the five-minute walk to the *Globe* offices, she decided that she had to call New York and talk to this woman.

When she arrived at the small, littered office, she hurried past the three reporters who were already at their desks, nodding good morning as they sifted through paper cups and napkins scattered in among the pages of stories in progress. Once at her desk, Kim Carlyle's number was easy to obtain, and, although it was 5:30 A.M. in New York, she made the transcontinental call. The phone rang four times and then a voice-mail message came on: "Hi, this is Kim Carlyle, I'm sorry I missed your call. But your call is important to me. Leave a message and number, and I'll get back to you at my earliest convenience."

Mariana knew little about Kim Carlyle, but she decided to be forward and direct with her. "This is Mariana Blair. I'm a news reporter for the *Globe*, the London newspaper," she said. "I was a friend of Brixton's—I'm sure you're aware of his death—and in light of what happened to your client in Los Angeles, I think we should talk. I have some information that might be useful to you. Please give me a call. I think we can help each other."

Mariana left her telephone number at the *Globe* and hung up.

Bill Wittington, her editor, approached just as she turned and began riffling through the stack of papers on her desk. He was an obese, frumpy man with a care-worn face. As usual his shirttail was hanging out of his trousers. "So, you decided to honor us with your company today," he said sarcastically.

"Yeah, sorry about that, Bill," she said, forcing a smile. "I'm on to something. I'll brief you in a few days."

"Nice of you to mention it, Mariana. It would be good if you made some time for the work that you've been assigned to do."

Mariana turned to her computer terminal. "Trust me, Bill. You're going to love this story," she said, her annoyance barely contained.

"Oh, I'm sure I will. So long as it's not another piece on these half-ass rap stars. I need something that grabs *our* audience, something on Jagger, McCartney, Rod Stewart, or Elton John—even Madonna or that Yank trollop J-Lo. Look at the *Mirror*. That's what we need."

Mariana again glanced at the photo of a glaze-eyed Britney Spears emerging from a club with just the hint of a nipple spilling from her halter top.

"Yes, Bill, I see what you mean. My story is not quite so, ah, *obvious*, but it's the biggest scoop this paper has ever had. Just give me some time to put it together, you'll see."

"That may be, but right now I need you for something . . . more obvious. There's a photographer waiting for you in the lobby. Get your pretty little bum over to Mayfair, and do what you do best. 'N Sync is staying at the Four Seasons Hotel and Eminem as well, with all that testosterone, something is bound to happen. If not, stir something up." He smiled knowingly and let his eyes travel from her modest bust to her face. "But first do something about those bags under your eyes; you look like you've been up for a week."

As Wittington turned and walked away, Mariana cursed him silently. A minute later, she grabbed a note pad and stalked out of the office.

It was near six o'clock when she returned to the *Globe*. As she expected, nothing much had happened at the hotel. Access to the floors on which the pop stars resided was sealed; she and many other reporters had spent the early afternoon sitting in a coffee shop watching bobbies trying to control the mob of teenagers outside the hotel. Two members of 'N Sync did surface briefly but allowed no interviews. They were whisked away in limousines while security fought off the screaming fans. Her photographer got a few shots of the mayhem but that was it.

She related all this to her editor and wearily turned to go back to her desk. "Who is Kim Carlyle?" Wittington asked, a Cheshire cat grin playing across his face.

"What—did she call?" Mariana asked, suddenly enlivened.

"Something to do with this story you're working on, I take it."

"Exactly—but did she call?"

"Yes, she called and left a cellphone number a few hours after you left. And there was another call from some guy at one of those swishy bars out on Old Brompton Road. He said you could find someone called the diamond cutter at The Lollie tonight." He paused, looking at her suspiciously. "What the hell's this all about, Mariana? What kind of cloak-and-dagger games are you playing?"

"It's no game, Bill," she said. "I don't want to go into details, but this is getting bigger than even I thought. I need some time, just a few days, and I'll tell you everything. I'll have enough to write the story."

"Okay, but just two days. I can't have you running around like a loose cannon representing the *Globe*." He tried to keep a stern look on his face, but she could see him softening. "Look, be careful out there; you sure you don't want some help?"

"No, Bill, this is my story; I can handle it."

She returned to her desk and, after a few minutes' thought, dialed Kim's number. The phone was picked up immediately, and she was greeted by an eager female voice on the other end of the line: "Hello, is this Mariana?"

Bill had followed her. When she noticed him standing near her desk, she pulled the phone from her ear and waved him away. She hated the way he lurked around reporters' desks when they were on the phone, and today she was determined not to be overheard. She waited until he retreated before speaking.

"Yes, is this Kim Carlyle?"

"Of course."

Mariana paused, hesitant to reveal too much but anxious to find out what Kim knew. "Look, I don't know you, but I've read that you're a former detective. So I'm sure that you've given some thought to the curious deaths of your clients Tiffany Jones and Cheeno."

"Curious? What, you're saying you have information on that?"

"I may have, and I don't think you know what it really involves. I was a friend of Brixton's, and I think his death was part of it as well. Then there were the deaths of Lester Bennett and Renee Rothchild; they may also be connected to this . . ." she paused again, to consider how much she should reveal.

"This what!" Kim demanded.

"All I can say with certainty now is that I have evidence that it's much more than some entertainment vendetta. Diamonds are apparently involved, and I think it's centered here—in England, Belgium, the Netherlands, and France—and it probably stretches much further. Everything points to—"

Mariana paused again when she noticed that Bill had returned and was standing behind her. She crouched her shoulders and lowered her voice to a whisper, "I can't really talk freely right now, but I'd like to find out what you know about Ruff Daddy and Tiffany's husband Klaus Svrenson. I don't know if it means much but they spent a lot of time in Amsterdam and both of them knew Kees Van derVall."

"Kees who . . . slow down," Kim said. "You're implicating a lot of people—making this sound like a major conspiracy. Do you have evidence?"

"Trust me, I know I'm on to something here, and, if you know anything, I could use your help getting to the bottom of it. You can ask questions, find out what's going on over there—these people were your friends, too. If you wish, I can even fly to New York."

"Wait, can't you tell me more now?"

"No. I have to hang up. I've said enough for now."

"Will you call later?"

"No, not tonight, there's something I have to do. But I'll call tomorrow."

"Mariana, wait—" Kim shouted as the phone clicked off.

"Damn it, Bill, I asked you to back off," Mariana said as she stood and angrily faced her editor. They argued for a minute before she turned, snatched her bag from the desk, and stormed toward the door shouting, "I'll see you tomorrow," over her shoulder.

Mariana stopped at her flat, made a few calls, and updated her notes before changing clothes and leaving for The Lollie. At the entrance, two burly black bouncers framed the door. The sound of funky house music blared behind them as they scanned the queue of about fifty people who stood outside the velvet ropes waving for their attention. Every five minutes or so, they pointed to someone and, after patting them down, allowed them to enter. Mariana stood in line for about ten minutes before moving toward the ropes and flashing her sexiest *Friends* smile. She had changed into high heels, a red Lagerfeld mini-skirt, and a sheer silk blouse that left little to the imagination. That was probably enough, but out of habit she flashed the press credentials that she carried in a small bag when one of the bouncers approached. Without hesitation, he opened the ropes and, after inspecting her bag, escorted her through the doors.

Inside, the hallway leading to the main room was noisy and crowded with shadowy figures pressed against the walls in intimate embraces. The faint smell of ganja drifted in the air. She started down the stairs toward the dim main floor when someone grabbed at her arm. Startled, she pulled away, but it was only a hostess stopping her to stamp her hand with an invisible brand indicating that she was among the chosen few who had been admitted.

Before stepping down onto the main floor of the huge hall, she took a deep breath and told herself to relax. She had decided that when she saw Freesley she would play it by ear. If the opportunity arose, she would approach and confront him. But she wouldn't press it, if she had to she would see whom he talked to and try to question them. She'd decided that if necessary she'd even follow Freesley home, find out where he lived, and use that information to step up her investigation.

She was still relatively new at this, and her mind was racing with possibilities. Her heart was pounding nearly as fast—it was part fear but there was also the thrill of living on the edge.

The dim smoke-filled dance floor was jam-packed with silhouetted figures writhing to the sound of "Fallin'" by Alicia Keyes. Standing at the top of the winding stairs leading to the heart of the thumping mix, Mariana peered down at the crowd. Under the flashing colored lights, it was nearly impossible to recognize anyone. She decided to head toward the long bar at the side of the hall; if Freesley was looking for her, she'd be easier to find there.

As she descended the stairs, a young woman in purple leather cigarette pants, an embroidered strapless top, and calf-high stiletto Gucci boots reeled back and forth, clinging to the banister ahead of her. Her long straight hair spilled forward concealing most of her face, which was covered with bizarre purple makeup. Suddenly, when Mariana tried to pass, the woman emerged from her apparent stupor and lurched forward.

"Happy New Year, deary," she muttered in a garbled Cockney-sounding accent as she embraced Mariana and tried to kiss her. Mariana quickly recoiled and, pushing her away, continued down the stairs. "Too good for me, you bloody bitch!" she heard from the stairwell as she elbowed her way onto the dance floor.

Despite her heels, she couldn't see anything but the dancers surrounding her as she pressed forward through the mob of hip-hop fanatics who bumped and rubbed against her. Snoop Dog's "Tha Last Meal" blared from the speakers, and, as she strained her neck to look for Freesley, she was also busy pushing away the sweaty hands that randomly swiped at her. When the song ended and the crowd slackened, she pushed ahead trying to make it to the bar before the lull ended. She was ten feet away from it when she felt a hot, ripping pain in her lower back. A gloved hand closed over her mouth as she fell back into someone's arms. The pain intensified, and she realized she was being dragged or carried backward toward the lounge chairs at the edge of the dance floor.

The room began to swim and the colored lights swirled above her as a curious calm settled over her. She tried to move her lips to speak but couldn't utter a word as she was lowered into one of the soft chairs. The old Naughty By Nature hit "O.P.P." came on at full blast, then faded as the swirling lights gradually stilled, dimmed, and darkened.

It was three hours later when a waiter finally discovered that the young woman in the Lagerfeld miniskirt who had been reclining in the corner of the lounge area for most of the night had not passed out and spilled a glass of red wine on her silk blouse as they had assumed. Mariana Blair was dead.

NINE

Las Vegas/New York—Tuesday, July 31

Las Vegas

"It's good! It's all good!" Brian Woods laughed as he hoisted a double shot of Grand Marnier and gulped it down. "Broads, booze, all the money, and, ah, accessories any *paesan* could want." He was sitting with three associates—Carmine "Linguini" Lozzi from Miami, Andy Anfuso from Los Angeles, and "Big Tony" Marintino from New York—in a large booth near the rear of the first floor bar at the Lucky Dragon Casino. Lozzi and Marintino watched with detached amusement as Woods flashed a broad, exaggerated smile and extended his hand out over the table to display manicured nails and a perfect two-and-a-half-carat diamond set in a platinum pinky ring.

"C'mon, drink up!" Woods urged. He waved for a red-haired waitress wearing a skimpy, low-cut outfit and net stockings, and reared back in his seat, fidgeting with the lapels of his slate-gray silk suit. As his eyes darted back and forth between the casino floor beyond the bar and the faces of the three men who sat with him, he drummed the fingers of his ringed hand on the table to the sound of the Al Martino ballad that filled the room. A rugged, good-looking thirty-nine-year-old, he had a reputation as a tough, fearlessly confident worker, but tonight his bravura seemed forced. Occasionally he dabbed at the small beads of sweat that uncharacteristically dripped from his dark, slicked-back hair onto the collar of his custom-made shirt.

He was the casino manager and second in command at The Dragon, a second-tier casino in Meadows Village about ten miles from the Las Vegas Strip. It was a run-down section of Vegas where you could rent a room in one of the seamy hotels for as little as $150 per month, less than the nightly rate at most of the plush casinos on the Strip. The Dragon masked its shoddy underside with glitzy accouterments and lighting, but, despite the veneer, it was mostly frequented by an odd assortment of hustlers, dyed-in-the-wool gamblers, and wanna-be wise guys. Tonight was an exception. Woods and his friend Anfuso, who had grown up in L.A. together after Woods's family moved from Ohio, were still trying to make their bones. But Marintino and Lozzi were made guys. In town "for a little recreation," they had offered, when they called from the MGM Grand, to drop by. They arrived wearing sandals, florid short-sleeved shirts, and slacks, which had somewhat eased Woods's anxiety about their sudden appearance.

"Last time I was in Detroit, your name came up," Lozzi said. He was a stocky, muscular man, and, when he pulled his arms back to rest them on top of the booth, his bulging biceps nearly ripped his shirt sleeve. "You know Victor Pasaro?"

"I was out there a few months ago, but we never met," Woods said. "Had to go to Warren on some business with Napolini's outfit, so I drove up to the Motor City. Not bad, not at all, but a few too many *molleres* for my taste. Know what I mean?"

"Damn right," Lozzi laughed, "motherfuckers multiply like rabbits."

"Yeah, but you got to use 'em these days if you wanna do business," Marintino laughed. "They got some heavy shit goin' on and we need to get our share. Fact is, we're thinkin' about settin' up our own record company in New York. There's a lotta money in this rap shit, and it don't cost nothin' to turn it out. Know what I mean?"

"Yeah, well, I don't know how you listen to that bullshit," Woods said. "But it don't matter, the guys out there got it under control. I was treated like a prince over at the Roma Café in the East Market district. No trouble, none at all. Whenever I travel, I try to pay my respects to the guys that already got their buttons. I know soldiers in Dallas, Chicago, Boston, New Orleans—all over the globe, even Brussels, Amsterdam, and *Milano*. Yeah, like I say, it's all good!"

Anfuso smiled and nodded in appreciation. The patronizing expression on Lozzi's face signaled that he was not impressed, and, when Marintino glanced at him, he averted his eyes and swirled his fork in the pasta marinara that accompanied his veal parmigiana. A moment later the buxom waitress arrived with shots of Jack Daniel's for Lozzi and Anfuso, and another double Grand Marnier for Woods. When she left, Lozzi turned and watched as she leaned over a nearby table to take an order. "Not bad," he said, half smiling. "Not bad at all."

"You want, *cugine*?" Woods said. "Just say the word, she's yours."

Lozzi turned back to the table. His smile faded as he shook his head and declined the invitation. Woods turned to Marintino.

"Tony, have some more *vino*," he gushed, picking up the bottle. "It's from my private stock, Brunello di Montalcino, 1989. Not like that swill they serve at the Grand."

Marintino smiled and nodded yes.

"Word is you brought some heavy action to Napolini," he said, after Woods filled his glass.

"Yeah, we're doin' some business," Woods said, beaming, "and it's just the beginning. I got plenty more—"

"How in the hell does an Italian get a name like Brian Woods?" Lozzi interrupted, a sarcastic grin on his face.

"*Sono italiano!*" Woods said emphatically.

"*Sei sicuro?*"

"Damn right I'm sure! I changed my name."

Lozzi's grin widened as Woods dabbed at his forehead with a cocktail napkin. He was enjoying every minute of the cocky upstart's discomfort.

"So, why'd you change your name?" Marintino asked.

"Lemme tell you," Woods said. "You know why I changed my name . . . I, ah, I used to work for a collection agency. I'd call these poor bastards—"

"Watch out, the bullshit's starting to fly," Lozzi laughed. He grabbed Marintino, winking as he hugged him. "This motherfucker's squirmin' like a stuck pig," he whispered.

"No! Wait a minute. Wait a minute! This is a true story," Woods said, anxious to save face.

"Yeah, like the Atlantic City story," Marintino said. "Atlantic City all over again."

"No, God's honest truth," Woods said. "I swear on my mother's grave."

Anfuso laughed, and for the first time during the evening spoke up. "Not for nothing, Brian, but your mother's not dead."

"Then on my grandmother's grave," Woods continued, without a hitch. "See, I'd call these mothers and tell them they better pay up— their phone bills, cable bills, whatever—if they knew what was good for them. You know, I'd suggest that if they didn't get the money immediately they might develop a serious knee problem—some crap like that. Anything to scare the fuck outta them. So this guy panics and takes me to court, I swear to God. Motherfucker took me to court. He tells the judge that I was threatening him—and, get this, trying to intimidate him by using an Italian name and pretending to be in the mob. . . . I swear to God. And the fucking Irish judge believed him. Cocksucker said that if I wanted to stay in the collection business I had to stop using my real name."

"So what happened to the pussy who complained," Marintino asked.

"I found him and busted his fucking knees—both of them," Woods laughed. "What the hell did you think I'd do?"

All four men were laughing now. In fact, Lozzi was holding his stomach trying to restrain himself, and Marintino, a huge, squat man who weighed nearly 250 pounds, was coughing and wheezing as he tried to catch his breath.

"So, what the hell is your real name?" Marintino finally asked.

Woods finished his drink and was about to answer when he stopped short. A tall graying man in sunglasses, impeccably dressed in shirt and tie and blue Brooks Brothers suit, was approaching them. Lozzi recognized him immediately and didn't seem surprised that he was there. He stood up, and the others followed his lead. When the man reached the table, Lozzi stepped forward to embrace him and kiss him on the cheek.

"Hi'ya doin', *cugine*," Lozzi said.

"You don't wanna know," the man said with a straight face, then he and Lozzi stepped back and laughed.

"Lemme introduce a friend of ours," Lozzi said.

It was Victor Pasaro, part of the Detroit outfit that shared control of the midwestern area, which included Michigan and Ohio. Marintino hugged and kissed Pasaro next and then Woods and Anfuso went through the ritual before the men sat back down.

"Seems like you guys were having a great time back here," Pasaro said. "What's so funny?"

"Ah, just bullshitting with Brian—talking about the old days," Marintino said.

"And what brings you to the bowels of Las Vegas?" Woods asked. "Don't you usually hang with the heavyweights over at The Sahara?" He picked up the Montalcino bottle and gestured toward the new arrival, silently offering him a drink. Pasaro nodded yes, then stopped him when the glass was half filled.

"That's good," he said, picking up the glass. "*Grazie*. It's early and I don't want to overdo it. I'm here on business. Napolini's crew sent me to assist you with the show that begins next week."

"What! Nobody said anything about it to me."

"Contact Riccardo if you want. He'll tell you himself."

"What the fuck is he thinking? This was my deal. I brought it to them, and I don't appreciate anyone stepping in and interfering!"

"Hey, *paesan*, calm down," Marintino said. "Don't get your dick hard when there's nothing to fuck. Listen to the man, it don't sound like nobody's taking anything away from you to me."

"Hell, no! This is mine. I took it to Riccardo because I knew him as a kid. I set up the whole diamond—"

Pasaro slammed his wineglass onto the table, nearly breaking it. "I'd be more careful about what the fuck I said if I was you," he growled.

"Yeah, I don't want no details," Marintino said.

Lozzi shook his head in disgust, pinning Woods with an icy gaze.

Anfuso shrunk back in his seat, visibly shaken. He was amazed that his friend had the balls to challenge a guy who'd already been straightened out. His eyes darted from Woods to Pasaro. Finally, Woods threw up his hands and called the waitress. He ordered another Grand Marnier.

"Yeah, you're right, *cugine*," he said to Pasaro. "We can talk later. It's six-thirty. I got time for one more drink before I start working tonight."

"Hey, Carmine," Marintino laughed, "why don't you tell them

about that fuck-up in Miami, when you guys popped the wrong Cuban chick and had to run for your lives from that gang of spics?"

"Hey, they all look alike, you know that. Well, maybe you don't. You New York guys are trying to be too . . . what's it called, *politically correct*. And anyway, we didn't run, we retreated until the next day and them came back and kicked ass."

"That ain't what I heard," Marintino laughed.

Woods had gotten his drink, and, after gulping it down, he sat glaring at Pasaro, visibly upset. The alcohol was taking its effect; he was not only high, he was stewing. Pasaro noticed and glared back at him for a minute, then stood up.

"Maybe we should talk now," he said.

"You know, I don't think we should talk at all," Woods said. "I was warned that something like this might happen. It's bullshit. I can take this deal somewhere else, you know. You're not the only family interested in making a fortune off diamonds. It's my deal."

"You know, Brian," Pasaro began. He paused and looked around the room. *"Tu serai un problemo. Tu parli troppo."*

"Che dici?"

Pasaro turned and started to walk away.

"Fuck you, Victor!" Woods yelled.

"Sono lava le mani," Pasaro said before leaving the table and walking to the bar.

Lozzi and Marintino immediately stood up. Marintino hugged Anfuso and, smiling, whispered something in his ear. Then both he and Lozzi hugged Woods before joining Pasaro, who had stopped at the bar and ordered a drink. They spoke for a few minutes before leaving.

"What the hell's goin' on," Anfuso asked Woods.

"Nothing . . . *nient!*"

Woods brushed pass Anfuso, heading for the casino floor. He paused briefly at Pasaro's side. "Look, don't you understand, it's my deal. I can handle it."

When Pasaro ignored him, he turned abruptly and walked away. Just as he stepped through the casino door, he heard the call from the bar. *"Tu sai nuotare?"* Pasaro shouted, before walking back toward the booth where Anfuso stood.

Woods made one run through the casino then started upstairs to the third-floor offices. He had decided to call Ohio and find out exactly why Pasaro was here. "Do you know how to swim?" was the last thing Pasaro had said to him. It was a clear threat, but Woods was fairly certain that Pasaro wouldn't try anything in the casino. There was too much security, and, besides, his boss Sal Palomo had big-time connections in Vegas and L.A., and he was upstairs. No, they wouldn't fuck with him in the casino, he assured himself.

Forty-five minutes after he left Pasaro in the bar, he stepped off the elevator on the third floor. The two security guards outside the elevator were at their stations. They nodded as he walked down the hallway past the counting room where three more heavily armed guards stood. When he reached Palomo's office, he paused outside, considering whether to confide in him. The old man was like a father to him.

He knocked and, when no one answered, pushed the door open and stepped inside. Palomo was slumped over his desk in the dimly lit room. A trickle of blood could be seen flowing onto the desk mat. Woods immediately reached inside his jacket and started to turn back toward the door. He never saw the gun and silencer that was shoved into the back of his head and, after the muted pop, hardly felt the bullet that ripped through the back of his skull.

New York

Kim Carlyle sat on her sofa with several pages of notes spread out on the coffee table. Both her telephone and cell lay beside her on the couch. For the last three hours she had intermittently paced nervously about the room or pored over the random notes she had made the previous night and earlier this morning while on the plane. Primarily she'd been waiting on a return call from the London reporter Mariana Blair. It was now almost ten o'clock—4:00 A.M. in England—and she had nearly given up hope of receiving the call. Still, she reminded herself, the woman had called and left a message at 5:00 A.M. New York time. It wasn't completely out of the question. The problem for Kim was her ten o'clock meeting with Lt. Jackson at the Sugar Bar.

At five minutes of ten, Kim gave up; she'd have to wait until the next morning to talk with the reporter. She slipped into designer jeans and a teal V-neck T-shirt, pushed her notes into a slim leather briefcase, and rushed out to get a cab. She quickly found one on West End Avenue and ten minutes later arrived at the 72nd Street restaurant. Lt. Jackson was just inside the door, sitting at the long bar that paralleled the narrow passageway leading to the downstairs restaurant. He was sipping a vodka and tonic and idly paging through the *Daily News* when she entered.

"Hi Maurice," she said as she sat down on the adjacent stool. "Thanks for meeting with me."

"You knew I couldn't turn down a beautiful woman in distress," he laughed, "even if she was once my biggest headache."

"Hey, if it wasn't for me, you would never have been promoted," she said. She ordered an apple martini, took a deep breath, and dug into her briefcase for her notes.

"So what's up, super sleuth? You've been worked up ever since this Tiffany thing—what's the deal? I thought you gave this crap up once you started hanging out with the beautiful people."

"Believe me, I thought I had too. Seems there are some things I can't get away from."

"Okay, I can understand your concern over the deaths of your friends, and, truthfully, the series of events seem a little peculiar to me also. In fact, I checked out the coroner's report on Tiffany's death myself."

"Yeah, did you find anything out of the ordinary?"

"Well, nothing conclusive. But there's certainly room for speculation. It was a diabetic seizure all right—set off by low blood sugar. Hypoglycemia, I think they call it. But it could have been caused by a number of things. Not all of them natural. An insulin overdose or, according to the coroner, even a drug like Pentamidine Isethionate could have set it off. The trouble is that the hypodermic needle that Tiffany carried was clean, no trace of any suspicious drugs, and Tiffany's husband claimed the body before we could do a truly thorough examination. As you know, he's got a lot of connections, and he used them. You also know she was cremated, right?"

"Yes, I was at the funeral."

"And unfortunately, since that rapper Cheeno died in L.A. and the other shooting occurred in Atlanta, there's not a helluva lot I can do about it. Not unless you've got something else—something that ties them together."

The bartender, a good-looking twenty-four-year-old black man who reminded Kim of Rick Dupre, set the martini before her and smiled suggestively. Probably another jive actor, she thought. Ignoring him, she turned back to Lt. Jackson.

"Until this morning, I didn't know squat—just a hunch, but as I told you this afternoon, I got a strange call from a reporter in London. She's convinced that there's some kind of plot going on. Something that goes way beyond Tiffany, Cheeno, and the English dude, Brixton. She's also talking about Lester Bennett, the jazz musician, and Renee Rothchild, the club owner in Paris."

"Yeah, I read about them," Lt. Jackson said, "but none of the papers indicated that those were suspicious deaths."

"I know. Still, there's something strange happening, Maurice.

Remember back in the day when we talked about *coincidence* and how you should always question it."

"Of course, but we also discussed how you had to get inside the chain of events and discover some logical motive that explained it. What do we have here—a plot to kill off black artists and return pop music to white folks?" He smiled condescendingly. "A little far-fetched, ain't it?"

"According to the reporter, it's not just music. There's more, much more," Kim said. She paused and, sipping the martini, considered just how much she should share with Lt. Jackson. The reporter had mentioned Ruff Daddy and Klaus, but she didn't want to cast any suspicion on them unless she was absolutely sure. Still, she had to give him something if she wanted his help.

"So, spit it out!" he said.

"Well, you ever heard of a hood named Kees Van derVall, from the Netherlands?"

Lt. Jackson shook his head no.

"He had his throat slit in a seedy hotel a few days after Tiffany died. This reporter, Mariana Blair from the *Globe*, thinks he's involved somehow. After I spoke to her, I did some research on-line. *De Telegraaf*, the Amsterdam paper, ran a long story on him. It seems that he was under investigation for everything from assault to drug peddling and murder. And Blair says he was also cozy with the mob here in the States as well as some American music honchos."

Lt. Jackson took a slug of his drink, then stared at the glass, a quizzical expression on his face. "So, you think the death of this guy Kees is somehow connected to the deaths of the entertainers?"

"I'm not sure, but . . . yes, I do."

"You got anything else, any evidence besides . . . your hunch, and the reporter's suspicions?"

"Nothing I could go to court with . . ." she paused, rubbing the top of her glass with an index finger. "But something's wrong, Maurice, I'm sure of it. And that reporter, I believe she's on to something. She sounded desperate."

Lt. Jackson grinned and slowly shook his head. "You know, I was always able to tell when you were holding something back. That's okay, you must have your reasons. But you gotta understand that I can't do anything officially with this kind of, ah, *evidence*. Look, if you're right—if the mob is involved in this and it's some international crime syndicate scheme—I'd have to go to my superiors and get the Organized Crime Control Bureau involved. And right now, with what you have, my boss would laugh and show me the door. You know what I'm sayin'?"

"Yes, I know. But that's not what I'm asking." Kim smiled and touched his shoulder. "You have resources that I don't have. What I need is for you to discreetly check out any information the OCCB has on Kees, find out who he knew in the States. And . . . well, see if he was smuggling anything besides heroin and guns."

"Like what?"

". . . Gems, specifically, diamonds."

Lt. Jackson raised his eyebrows and stared at her. "Sure you don't want to tell me more about this?"

"Maurice, when I'm certain, I will. You know that." She rose and, again, touched his shoulder. "Do this for me, okay?"

She turned, excused herself, and walked through the narrow aisle leading to the rest rooms near the rear of the restaurant. The cozy indoor room at the back, decorated with African paintings and sculpture, was nearly filled, and the canopied outdoor space was packed. She nodded at a couple sitting inside and waved at a young actor who sat alone at another table. As usual, the upscale crowd was dotted with entertainers. The Sugar Bar was owned by Ashford and Simpson, the recording and song-writing team, and legendary performers like Isaac Hayes and James Brown were known to drop in occasionally. It was not only one of Kim's favorite restaurants but also an excellent spot for networking and getting the skinny on any hot, new performers. Tonight, however, she had other things on her mind. She entered the ladies' room without stopping to speak to anyone.

When she returned to the bar, Lt. Jackson had finished his drink and sat fingering an unlit cigarette—something Kim had only seen him do when he was disturbed or struggling to solve some puzzle.

"Got to go," he said; "I'm on duty very early tomorrow." He stood and reached for the check.

"No way," Kim said, "I know what they pay you guys. This is on me."

"I'm not arguing with that," he said as Kim paid the check.

Outside, standing near his unmarked car, Lt. Jackson offered her a lift home but she declined, saying she wanted to walk. When she turned to leave, Lt. Jackson shouted to get her attention.

"Hey! There is one thing you might like to know. But first I want you to promise that you'll keep me updated on this whole thing. I got an uneasy feeling about it myself, but, like I said, I can't do anything officially with what's on the table now."

"You got it," she said. "But what is it you wanted to tell me?"

"For what it's worth—and I'm not sure it means anything—after you left the Apollo the night Tiffany died, her husband came back. He wanted to take Tiffany's jewelry, the rings and the huge diamond pendant she was wearing. We told him that nothing could be removed from the body at that time, and he went off—pitched a bitch then stormed out again, you know what I mean. Later, I heard that one of the detectives who knew a little about precious gems had looked at the pendant and insisted it was a fake. But Klaus went to the coroner's office the next morning and got the jewelry. He had permission to pick up her belongings. It just struck me as peculiar that anyone would be that interested in retrieving some worthless cut glass."

"Yes," Kim said, fighting to conceal her real concern, "more than strange."

Lt. Jackson smiled and stared at her until she averted her eyes. "We've known each other for a long time," he said, "and I know you're not telling me everything. It's okay—for now, but don't let this get out of hand. I'll see what I can do. Call me tomorrow, and be careful."

Kim crossed the street, turned at Broadway, and began the long hike back to 99th Street. Nearly all her thoughts revolved around Klaus Svrenson. Could he be a key player in some worldwide scheme involving diamonds? Was he involved in his own wife's death? How well did he know her friend Ruff Daddy? And where had he gone?

Maybe tomorrow she would get some answers from Mariana Blair, she thought, as she wove through the pedestrians who still streamed along Broadway on this humid Manhattan night.

Further uptown, at the corner of 119th Street and Malcolm X Boulevard in Harlem, a hefty, balding man with shining ebony skin turned out the lights, locked up, and placed a closed sign on the glass door of the Old World Music Shop. As Clarence "Mojo" Johnson peered out at a group of teenagers loitering on the corner across the street, his towering frame, draped in a blue West African shirt-suit, all but blocked the doorway. Moments later he looked at his watch, turned, and made his way back through the darkened store.

He didn't need lights. He knew the contours of the room like he knew his own body. He didn't trip or falter as he eased around bins and boxes crammed with LPs and old 78 and 45 platters. Most people thought of his shop as a shoddy secondhand store—nothing more than a blemish on Harlem's rapidly gentrifying face. In fact, it had been exactly that up until about a year ago.

While Mojo had done little to improve its outward appearance during the past year, he had radically upgraded and expanded the store's inventory. It was now a treasure chest of unusual, extremely rare recordings, which had been shipped to him from locations throughout America as well as from points in the West Indies and Africa. Discerning music collectors knew that Mojo owned many priceless vinyl singles and albums—original gospel, reggae, world beat, blues, and jazz recordings that had experts shaking their heads with wonder. And during the day, it was not unusual to see a stream of well-heeled downtown patrons mingling with Harlemites who browsed through the stock or stepped into the back room to confer with Mojo. No one knew exactly how he had managed to obtain them, but Mojo had somehow acquired vintage phonograph records that many had claimed no longer existed.

At the rear of the store, he pushed through the door leading to the small stockroom and office. He locked the door, brushed past the desk and safe, and moved to the far wall. Behind a heavy curtain was a second door; Mojo opened it and stepped into the hidden space behind it. He bolted the door before switching on the single overhead light.

Although somewhat larger than the stockroom, it was a cramped, unkempt space with a dirt floor and, except for a wooden shelf with about three dozen bottles on it, bare cement walls. Inside the bottles were exotic oddities such as dogs' fangs, alligators' teeth, crushed glass, and parrots' beaks. A brown rooster strutted back and forth in a wire cage in the corner to Mojo's left and, in front of him, adjacent to the rooster, were three glass cages. The first contained two tarantulas: one male and one female. An iguana sat motionless in the second cage. The third was empty. At the rear was a heavily bolted door.

Mojo smiled, closed his eyes, and silently began to pray.

Moments later, he heard the coded pounding on the rear door. The members and new recruits had arrived. Mojo opened the door and stepped back, allowing the dozen or so men who stood outside to enter. He greeted the members, each of whom had brought a recruit, as they filed inside. Frowning, he stepped outside and scanned the empty lot and two crumbling, abandoned buildings that surrounded it. A few addicts huddled in one of the buildings to the left, but no one was visible. Angrily, he slammed the door, double-bolted it, and turned toward the men who had entered. They stood at attention, awaiting his instructions.

"Welcome, brothers," Mojo said, "let us pray."

The men kneeled in a circle at the center of the room, bowing their heads. Within minutes, most drifted into a meditative, trancelike state. Twenty minutes later, the silence was interrupted by another knock at the door. None of the new arrivals moved. It was only when the pounding became more insistent that Mojo stirred, slowly opening his eyes and exhaling. He rose, quietly stood up, and moved toward the bolted door.

Waiting outside was a slight, sinewy man with long dreadlocks. It was Martin Latrell, second in command in the sect. His rimless glasses were perched low on his nose, and, despite his cream-colored wool trousers and tan turtleneck, he seemed cool and relaxed.

"Where have you been, brother?" Mojo said sternly. "You knew what time we started."

"Sorry," Latrell said, brushing past Mojo and entering the dimly lit room. "I was detained."

Mojo stiffened at the curt response but didn't reply. With conscious restraint he led Latrell to a spot near the center of the circle where they both knelt without interrupting the others.

After five more minutes of silent meditation, Mojo rose. "We can begin now," he said quietly.

The men stood, and Mojo walked over to the shelf. In a bowl that sat on a simple pine table below the shelf, Mojo carefully mixed a mound of gunpowder with a handful of dirt that was supposed to have come from a freshly dug grave. He returned to the circle of men, holding the bowl in one hand and a straight-edged barber's razor in the other.

Each man held out an arm. Mojo went around the circle and, one by one, made a small cut on each man's hand just deep enough for blood to trickle freely into the bowl. After Latrell submitted to the ritual, Mojo carefully sliced his own hand and watched as his blood dripped into the mixture.

A moment later, he set the bowl down in the center of the circle and began slowly stirring it as he recited the traditional Obeah incantation. With closed eyes, the men repeated the words after each pause. Once again they drifted into a near trance. Latrell was the only one who refrained. Feigning reverence, he scanned the kneeling figures before him with calculated detachment. He knew according to Obeah belief his behavior was a sacrilege. He also knew that Mojo and the others were almost fanatical believers. Even the new recruits were carefully checked before being invited to the meetings. When he joined, Latrell had also believed in the spirit and goals of the sect as well as in the dire consequences that the Orishas would visit on those who violated the confidence of the rituals or betrayed any other member. He had in the last year, however, adopted a much more secular viewpoint. And it was Mojo who had unintentionally spurred his disavowal.

Latrell closed his eyes when Mojo rose and moved to the pine table where he picked up another, larger wooden bowl before returning to the circle. In the center of the bowl sat a concrete, cone-shaped figurine with cowrie shells for eyes and a mouth. He placed the bowl in the center of the circle before walking over to the wire cage that held the rooster. Mojo lifted the hatch and carried the bird back to the circle. Raising the animal high up over his head, Mojo solemnly chanted out a prayer of thanks and obedience to Elegua, the mischievous spirit of fifty-six faces, the god of the crossroads.

Then he kneeled over the bowl and, with the same bloodied razor that had been used on the members, cut the rooster's throat and drained its blood into the bowl. Mojo seemed unaware of the dying bird's bucking and thrashing in his thick arms. All of the witnesses save Latrell—who faked entrancement and observed through narrowed eyes—chanted and prayed as fervently as Mojo.

When Mojo finished and again kneeled in prayer, two of the senior

brothers rose and removed the bowls before returning to their positions in the circle. Latrell then rose and returned with another, empty
bowl, which was placed at the center of the circle. Mojo rose and, with
eyes sparkling feverishly, began mumbling under his breath and ges-
turing wildly. His dark, calloused hands cut through the air menacingly as he paced in circles. He was completely unaware of anything
around him. Latrell stared at him blankly, trying to mask his cynicism
and contempt.

Mojo strode over to the glass case containing the tarantulas, took
out the female spider, and carried it back to the circle. She was much
larger and fatter than her companion. The sluggish, hairy spider was
monstrously big, nearly the size of Mojo's two massive hands cupped
together. The hairs bristled on the spider's long, black-tipped legs as
Mojo flipped her upside down and plunged his razor into the spider's
thorax.

With expertise, he severed the spider's venom sack and poured the
thick liquid into his bowl. He stepped back and raised his hands, an
almost beatific glow on his face.

"I am Mojo. I am Obi-man. I call on you, Bones, King of Death, to
intercede on my behalf against my enemies. I call on you, Oduda, you
who guides and sets my path. I have been wronged. I have been mis-
used. My enemies have poisoned my life with their wicked, sinful
ways, and I call on you to respond in kind, my gods. Avenge me against
those who would hinder my path and keep me from my treasures that
I would use to glorify your names and the names of our people. I give
myself over to you, body and soul. Avenge me against those false and
covetous enough to attempt to stop our work. Hear me, all powerful
Oduda!"

The ceremony continued late into the night. When Mojo finished,
satisfied that the recruits were thoroughly impressed and that the gods
had heard his pleas and would respond favorably, he dispersed the

meeting. The men were led to the table where they ceremoniously dipped their fingers into each of the bowls, bowed, and prayed. After toweling off the rancid mixtures, the men were escorted to the door, where each paused and thanked Mojo before marching out into the dark Harlem night.

Latrell stayed behind.

"Martin, we need to talk," Mojo said when the door had been bolted and secured. "I could feel the distance tonight."

"I don't know what you're talkin' about," Martin said, staring defiantly up into Mojo's eyes.

"I think you do, my brother," Mojo said, before pausing and shaking his head. "Back when we first met, you were just a flunky serving the white devils, a gofer collecting crumbs for Shabazz Pearson. Shabazz is a traitor to our people, Martin. You knew it then, and nothing has changed. He's dealing crack and running numbers, destroying our community. But I pulled you out of that. I selected you as my assistant because I sensed that you were a strong, capable black man. I also believed that you shared my vision for our people. It pains me to think that you may be backsliding, that you're losing the faith. Do you want to return to treading on the backs of our people, scrounging nickels from poor black souls who persist in the belief that drugs or a few dollars will somehow save or deliver them? Martin, I've opened my heart to you, tried to elevate you spiritually as well as financially so that you might take part in the greater cause. I trusted you, my brother. I hope that you haven't betrayed that trust, defamed my . . . no, our sanctuary. The Orishas see into your heart. They know the things that you're too fearful to reveal to me."

Latrell stared into Mojo's eyes, which were now dilated and flushed with the same intensity witnessed during the ceremony; he tried desperately to restrain himself. "Clarence," he said, after a long pause, "you know I appreciate you giving me the chance to join you in the struggle. I'm your righteous servant, you know that, brother. Any disrespect you may have felt tonight was unintended. I may drift sometimes, but it's only because I'm so involved with the details of our, uh, operation. I—"

"The Orishas do not lie, Martin. I hope you understand that no act of heresy, no pretense will be tolerated." He paused.

"Clarence, I ain't nobody's fool. I know what you've done for me." He patted his pocket, visibly bulging with a fat roll of bills, and touched the diamond-studded bracelet that hung from his wrist. "But when you brought me in, brother, you knew I was from the streets. Yeah, I'm strugglin', tryin' to deal with the spiritual side, but I'm with you till the end."

"We'll see, Martin. But I don't want to be misled. I too have powerful contacts on the streets, considerably more powerful than Shabazz. Nothing you do is unseen. Don't ever think your childish pretense goes unnoticed." Mojo turned, went to the pine table, and picked up one of the wooden bowls. He carefully poured it into a drain in the corner of the room. After emptying the other two bowls, he turned on the spigot above the drain. "I'll be watching you, Martin. But, more importantly, the Orishas are watching. Don't disappoint me."

Latrell steeled himself as Mojo rose and walked toward him. The huge man stopped a few feet away from him, towering above and staring into his eyes, searching for some sign of his true feelings. "You are growing in spirit, Martin, but you're still an infidel. I hope that soon you'll see the light, accept the will of Obeah. Remember, we are only instruments in the hands of Elegua, who requires our strict obedience."

Mojo turned and unbolted the door leading to the office and storage space. "Come," he said, "we have work to do. There are several packages that must be prepared and delivered by tomorrow morning."

"Hypocrite," Latrell muttered under his breath as he followed Mojo into the office. Inside, however, he smiled benignly as the two men pried open a crate, marked PHONOGRAPH RECORDINGS/HANDLE WITH

CARE, that had arrived from Africa and been ushered through John F. Kennedy Airport customs by several well-placed airport workers earlier that morning. Latrell's eyes widened when Mojo carefully removed a small cloth sack filled with gems from inside the otherwise empty slip of a vintage Miriam Makeba album cover.

TEN

NEW YORK—WEDNESDAY, AUGUST 1

The second call Kim Carlyle received on Wednesday morning came as she stood in her kitchen. She was impatiently waiting for the pot of Afra Gourmet Coffee to finish brewing when the phone rang. The first call had been from Rick Dupre, who awakened her from a sound sleep; she had reluctantly agreed to meet him for dinner later that evening at the Sugar Bar. Now, she hastily poured a cup of the imported African brew, went to the living room, and picked up the phone. It was Lt. Jackson, and, when she heard his voice, she knew something was wrong. No jokes—none of the usual frivolous repartee. He came directly to the point.

"What was the name of the reporter who called you from London?" he asked.

"Blair, Mariana Blair," she said. "Why? Did you receive some information about her?"

"Yeah, I'm afraid so—she's dead. Murdered in some trendy joint in London last night."

"What! Are you sure that it was the *Globe* reporter?"

"Without doubt—unless they've got another with the same name. It's all over the British tabloids. Some are playing it up as a lurid sex killing. Seems one of the bouncers saw her arguing with a bizarre unidentified woman who approached her just before she was stabbed."

Kim took the phone from her ear and breathed deeply. Damn, she thought, shaking her head. I'm caught in the middle of some international intrigue, and I don't even know what it's all about.

"Are you there? Hello, are you still there?" Lt. Jackson was shouting when she returned the receiver to her ear.

"Yes, yes, I'm here."

"Look, Kim," he said, "I'll tell you the truth; I was skeptical about your conspiracy theory at first, but now . . . well, I don't know. But I do know you well enough to know you're not telling me everything. And, friend or not, if you're hiding evidence about what could be a murder in my jurisdiction, I can't be responsible for what happens to you. Bottom line is, I need to know everything you know about this—today!"

"Okay, okay Maurice, I agree this is getting out of hand. I'm going to take the day off. Can you meet me for coffee at Henry's a little later?"

"Twelve o'clock all right?"

"I'll be there."

When Lt. Jackson hung up, Kim immediately called the *Globe*.

Bill Wittington's secretary answered, and a few seconds later the obviously shaken editor picked up the phone.

"Hello, Miss Carlyle?"

"Yes, it's Kim Carlyle," she said. "Is it true that Mariana Blair was murdered last night?"

"I'm afraid so—"

"Well, what's this about a sexual tryst—are you sure her death didn't have something to do with the story she was working on for your paper?"

"The sex stuff is tabloid hype," he said before pausing and taking a deep breath. "Look, Miss Carlyle, you're one of the last people Mariana talked to before she left the office last night—what did she say to you? Do you have any information?"

"I was going to ask you the same thing. She hung up in the middle of the call before telling me much of anything. She mentioned a few people who she thought were involved in some diamond scam, but that was it. Was that the story she was writing?"

"First, let me ask you something. How do I know you're not involved in this thing yourself?"

"You don't, Mr. Wittington! All I can tell you is that before yesterday I'd never heard of Mariana Blair. She called me out of the blue and began suggesting that the recent deaths of some musical performers in the United States—including two of my clients, Tiffany Jones and Cheeno—were connected to something that was going on in Europe. She worked for your paper; you must know something about it."

There was a moment of silence on Wittington's end of the line. "All right," he said finally. "Let me be more forthright. When I heard that Mariana had been killed, I immediately ran a check on you. I know you're a former New York detective, and it appears you're on the up and up. I'll tell you what little I know if you'll do the same. Do we have a deal?"

"Yes, of course. The important thing is to get to the bottom of all this."

"That's important all right, but remember I'm a newsman, and this was to be our story, you know. I'll work with you if you'll help me."

"Fine, just tell me what you know," she said sharply.

"Actually Mariana was extremely secretive; she refused to give me any details. She wanted to break the story herself, but I believe she went to that club to meet someone who she thought was an informant.

And the diamond angle makes sense. Before she left, she received a call saying she was to meet someone called the "diamond cutter." I have no idea who that is, not yet. And I don't know what Tiffany Jones or that rapper Cheeno has to do with this, but I do know she had been seeing a lot of Brixton. Also she had some of our stringers checking on the activities of a Dutch hoodlum named Van derVall. Maybe it's all connected. That's all I know, and this morning I related that information to the constable who questioned me."

"That's it, that's all you know?"

"That's everything, except that when the authorities searched her flat this morning they found it ransacked—turned inside out."

"Did the police find anything?"

"Not really, not even her notes. If she left anything behind, it appears that someone got to it before they arrived."

"But she must have had notes . . . something."

"Maybe, but what about you, did she tell you anything? I'd like to know before Scotland Yard calls you."

"Scotland Yard?"

"Yes, I had to give them your name. As I said, you were one of the last to speak to her. So! Why was she so anxious to talk to you?"

Again, Kim hesitated. She was still reluctant to bring up Ruff Daddy and Klaus Svrenson until she was absolutely sure they were involved. And if Wittington wasn't lying, the names hadn't come up yet.

"As I said, she wasn't very forthcoming. She wanted me to look into possible connections between the deaths of my clients and the deaths of Brixton and the two musicians from France, Lester Bennett and Renee Rothchild. And, yes . . . she mentioned Kees Van derVall, she seemed certain he had been involved in some way."

"Did you know Brixton or Bennett and Rothchild?"

"No."

"What about this guy Ruff Daddy? The rap mogul who invited Brixton to America. Did she mention him?"

"Er, no . . . why, does he have something to do with it?"

"I'm not sure, but Mariana did a story on him a while back and she liked to consort with these black musicians," he said, attempting to provoke her into revealing something more.

"I'm sure there was a very good reason for her preference," Kim snapped. "You sure there's nothing else?"

"Miss Carlyle, I'm a newsman," he said, getting more annoyed with her reticence. "We're still working on this but there is only so much I'm willing to divulge. Read tomorrow's edition."

"I'll do that," Kim said. Then, softening her voice, she added: "If I find something concrete, I'll contact you, for Mariana's sake. This was her story, and I guess she would have wanted the *Globe* to have it."

She hung up, more frustrated than before she called. Wittington either wasn't saying anything or knew nothing. And if he wasn't lying about Scotland Yard, they didn't know much more.

Before finishing her coffee and going upstairs to dress for the meeting with Lt. Jackson, Kim tried once again to call Klaus Svrenson at his home and office, and Ruff Daddy at his office and on his cell. Neither could be reached. She left messages with their assistants as well as on their machines, then she put aside her frustration and began preparing herself to face her old friend's interrogation.

At Henry's, Kim told Lt. Jackson everything, or at least everything she was absolutely certain about. That, of course, allowed her to avoid mention of Mariana Blair's suspicions about Ruff Daddy and Klaus. She did, however, air her concern about their dropping out of sight and about the mysterious disappearance of Maria Casells, as well as what she knew about the musicians who had died in France. She also told him all she knew about Cheeno and the unknown patron who had apparently been supporting him, and repeated what the *Globe* editor had said about Blair's intended rendezvous with the "diamond cutter" on the night of her death.

Both agreed that all evidence pointed toward some crooked diamond scheme. But that didn't explain the deaths of the musicians. Neither could figure out exactly how or even if they were involved. And if they were part of it, why were they being killed and who was doing it?

The only new information Lt. Jackson offered came from some discreet inquiries made with the OCCB regarding Kees Van derVall. The Bureau knew that Van derVall had been in the United States at least once and had spent his time in New York City and Cleveland. In the larger picture, he was considered small time. The detective seemed far more interested in the whereabouts of Klaus Svrenson. Based on Klaus's curious interest in the fake jewelry Tiffany was wearing and his disappearance after her death, and on the English reporter's having gone to meet someone from the diamond industry, Lt. Jackson had made Svrenson one of his central concerns. "It's not very much to go on," he said, "but Klaus is the only apparent link between the deaths and the diamonds." When they paid the check, he told Kim that, for the time being, he'd direct his efforts at finding and questioning Tiffany's husband.

It was nearly 2:30 when she left the restaurant at 103rd Street and Broadway and walked back to her apartment. A half hour after returning home, Kim received her third call of the day. It was Ruff Daddy phoning on his cell.

"Hey, baby," he said, "it's me, Ruff."

"Shelton," she gasped, "where are you? Are you all right?"

"Yeah, of course. I'm just layin' low till all this shit blows over."

"I've been trying to contact you for over a week. What the hell is going on? I . . . I thought something had happened to you. Why did you suddenly drop out of sight and . . . well, do you know anything about these killings?"

"That's why I'm calling, Kim. Fact is, I'm in this shit up to my ass.

And, if my info is correct, you already know a whole lot about what's going on. Thing is, I had to disappear to protect myself. Niggas droppin' like flies out here—you know what I'm sayin'? I still don't know if that Atlanta hit was intended for me or Brixton. I need your help, baby—and, well, I'm willing to help you too."

"What exactly are you involved in, Shelton? And who's after you and the others?"

"First tip is my involvement is between me and my lawyers. And if I knew who was poppin' these dudes I'd a done something about it myself. Which gets us back to the real deal. I know you were in touch with Mariana Blair before she got iced and you working with this detective, Jackson, from the Twenty-eighth. But from what I hear y'all been chasin' your tails. I'm lookin' out for my own ass, that's why I'm willing to help. If you'll look out for my interests, I can point you in the right direction. Is that cool?"

"You know I can't promise to protect you—not unless I know how deeply you're involved in all this."

"Yeah, well, I thought you might go that route. Always on the straight and narrow, ain't you?"

Kim didn't answer.

"Don't matter, I'll look out for myself. What I can tell you is that nobody involved in the deal—"

"What the hell is *the deal*?"

"C'mon, sugar, don't be coy. I know that you and Jackson figured out that this whole thing is about diamonds."

"Okay, that's true. We suspected that much, but how—"

"Forget it, baby. I ain't implicating myself, and like I said nobody knows the whole picture, except maybe Klaus Svrenson."

"Klaus *is* involved then?"

"Yeah, but I don't believe he's the one responsible for the death of his wife and the others. Far as I could tell, he ain't got the balls. No, it's much bigger than that, and whoever's doin' it got real muscle behind them."

"Shelton, how can I possibly help if you don't tell me any more than this?"

"Like I said, I only know parts of the operation and I can point you in that direction. Everybody I know is either dead or running scared."

"All right, I won't ask any more questions now," Kim said; Ruff Daddy wouldn't be coerced. "Where should I start looking?"

"There're a couple of things. First I don't know what's up with Mo; I ain't heard from the nigga since the drive-by. Ain't like him, he would've left a message unless he's hidin' something and duckin' me. I'd also have your detective friend look into the death of K. J. Hunter, that Texas businessman, and if I were you I'd check out that Atlanta detective Freddy Carmichael. Something strange about that dude. He was suppose to be on the case, protectin' us."

"No way, Freddy's all right—"

"I ain't sure about that, but it's up to you. I do know that there's a broad in New Orleans, Josephine St. Claire, who was at the center of everything. She wasn't runnin' the show, but she was key. Some of the art work she imported was more valuable than she let on. You know what I'm sayin'?"

The name sounded familiar. And, after a moment's thought, Kim realized that though she didn't know St. Claire, Tiffany Jones had known her and occasionally talked about her, even shown her pictures. Tiffany had been the guest of honor at a few lavish parties thrown by the woman. Kim had been invited to attend once or twice, but she'd always declined.

"How do I find her?"

"Easy, she owns a big-time art gallery down there and has connections all over Europe and Africa. And . . . well, there's one other thing." Ruff Daddy paused, in thought.

"Yeah, what is it?"

"What you doin' tonight? There're some people I want you to see."

"I was supposed to meet Rick at the Sugar Bar for dinner at nine, but I guess I can postpone it."

"No need, but can you meet him at the Lenox Lounge? Then I could meet you a half hour earlier."

"So you're in town?"

"Back off with the detective bullshit—can you meet me there?"

"Yes, of course, but—"

"Don't be late, and, Kim, don't bring your cop friend with you if you want to see me, understand? And take your cellphone in case I need to call you," Ruff Daddy said before hanging up.

She immediately called Rick Dupre and changed the site of their dinner date.

It was 8:15 when Kim stepped out of a cab in front of the Lenox Lounge. Her haute couture Joseph Abboud skirt and silk blouse were contrasted sharply with the attire of most pedestrians who traipsed between 124th and 125th Streets and with the commonplace appearance of the supper club itself. The Lounge, which opened in 1939, was a historical Harlem landmark, and the new owners had insisted on maintaining its original appearance. So outside, with its dull-red exterior and the large block lettering, it did not stand out from the surrounding buildings, having the faded look of a 1940s speakeasy. Inside, however, the original art deco interior had been preserved and restored to its former glory. Kim's chic attire was perfectly suited to the decor and the upscale dress of most of the other patrons, both locals and the new influx of downtown visitors and tourists.

She quickly scanned the bar to her left and the booths to her right when she entered, hoping that Ruff Daddy had already arrived. She also looked into the Zebra Room, and at the bandstand and dining area in the back of the restaurant, before taking a seat at the bar to wait for him. Kim ordered a martini and politely informed two admirers that she was waiting for her date. Her cell rang fifteen minutes later. It was Ruff Daddy.

"Hey, I see you made it," she heard him say over the buzz of conversation at the bar.

"Yes, I did. Where are you?"

"Don't matter," he said. "The important thing is that you're there. Do you have a clear view of the booths near the front window?"

Kim looked over her shoulder at lounge booths. "Yes, I'm at the bar, near the door. I can see them."

"Okay. And is there a big, heavyset dude with a balding head sitting in the corner booth?"

"Yeeessss," she said, becoming increasingly impatient.

"I thought he'd be there tonight. That's Clarence Johnson, better known as Mojo, and he should be sitting with a tall African dude who usually wears a dashiki."

"Right again, but what's all this supposed to mean?"

"Well, that's Ezekiel Kwabena, a businessman from Sierra Leone who's connected all the way up to the U.S. Congress. You wanted information on this diamond deal, well, it's sitting right in front of you. Except for Klaus—and I don't know where the hell he is—they're the only two people I know in the deal who are still breathing. They're also the reason I didn't show up tonight. I ain't taking no chances until I find out who's behind this shit."

"I don't know this Kwa . . . Kwabena, but isn't Clarence Johnson the owner of a record shop up here?"

"Right, and how do you think that rat hole, secondhand store got to be so successful in the last year or so?"

Kim paused, staring at the two men who laughed heartily as they devoured the southern-style seafood dishes they had ordered.

"That's it, baby. I've given you all I know right now. I'm working on this as hard as you. Hot diamonds are one thing, murder is something else—particularly when the killer ain't showin' his face and I stand a chance of gettin' popped."

"Shelton, you know I can't hide this, I mean your involvement, from Lt. Jackson, don't you?"

"Yeah, but don't worry, I don't expect anything less. I don't mind dealing with this diamond thing—shit, I was just a high-priced courier. My lawyers have me out on the street before Eminem release another one of his lame-ass CDs. But I don't intend to go down for no murder rap that I didn't do. I got plans, big plans. Look, if I get anything else, I'll call. And don't bother looking, you won't find me," he said before hanging up.

"Wait a minute," she yelled, then slammed the phone shut. After a moment's thought, she dialed the precinct. Lt. Jackson wasn't there, but she left an urgent message for him to call her. After sliding her phone back into her bag, she turned toward the corner booth. She had to calm herself because her first impulse was to confront the pair. If Ruff Daddy had been telling the truth, she was sitting forty feet away from two felons and possible murderers. She took a sip from her barely touched martini and drew a deep breath. On the other hand, they could just as well be the next victims, or there was the possibility that Ruff Daddy was lying. After a few moments' thought, she settled herself. No matter what, they weren't going anywhere and she didn't have any real evidence. All she could really do was tell Lt. Jackson, and, if he believed Ruff Daddy's allegations, perhaps he'd put them under surveillance. That decided, she still couldn't resist an occasional quick glance at Mojo and Kwabena.

It was a little after nine when Rick Dupre entered but before Kim could get his attention, he spotted Mojo and walked over to the booth. She watched as Mojo greeted him as if they were old friends, then gestured toward Kwabena, introducing him to Rick. Kwabena stood and shook his hand, and the three men talked for a few minutes before Rick turned and saw Kim at the bar.

He quickly approached her.

"Hey, sorry I'm late," he said, bending to kiss her on the cheek. "Couldn't find a spot."

"That's okay, but who are the guys in the booth? Somebody you know?"

"Everybody knows Mojo. He owns the Old World Music Shop on 119th Street. Got the best old jams in New York. The other guy is from Africa, a business associate. Why, looking for new clients?"

"No, but they look rather interesting. Want to introduce me?"

"It's not the best time, they're talking business now and the African dude, Kwo-Kwabena, has an early flight back to Freetown tomorrow. Besides, it's been a long time. I need to talk to you." He laughed and, taking her hand, led her back toward the dining room.

Kim hesitantly followed, nervously glancing over her shoulder as they moved through the crowded bar. When they reached the Zebra Room, she relaxed a bit despite her concern about Mojo and the African. The fabled jazz lounge had hosted performances by jazz greats ranging from Billie Holiday and Miles Davis to Branford Marsalis and Terrence Blanchard. And Harlem luminaries from Bill "Bojangles" Robinson and Malcolm X to Representative Charles Rangel and former President Bill Clinton had listened to sounds or dined there. Kim had always felt a sense of exultation when she entered the room, and tonight was no different.

They were seated close to the bandstand and grand piano where John Hicks and his trio had just started their first set. Kim didn't hear much of the music because Rick spent most of the set trying to explain why he had left her place on the night of Tiffany's death and why he'd been arrested at an after-hours club. They were halfway through their meal and the set had ended when he noticed that she wasn't really listening.

"Damn, baby, I'm here pouring my heart out and your head is

somewhere else. What's goin' on, I thought we here trying to patch things up?"

"Sorry, Rick," she said, snapping back from her own thoughts. "I'm a little preoccupied." She reached out and touched his hand.

"Look, why don't we get outta here and cruise by your place?" he said.

Kim had turned back toward the lounge and was peering at the two men who still sat in the corner when she felt Rick pull at her hand. "Oh, what did you say?"

"Nothing, baby. Forget it."

"Uh . . . how did you meet Mojo?" she asked.

"Mojo? We still on that? Look, he ain't nothin' but a hustler far as I know. He got the record shop and he runs some kinda self-improvement cult. Got a whole lot of niggas believing they can get in touch with the spirit and improve themselves if they join him. I think it's some kinda voodoo or—Obeah, I think that's what he calls it. Too much like that L. Ron Hubbard thing for me.

"Shit might work though, I know a few actors and performers who joined, and every one of them seem to get themselves together right afterward. Some couldn't get a job no way, and suddenly they were flying off to Europe and Africa for gigs and returning with deep pockets. I thought about it, but, no, it ain't my thing. I ain't jettin' to Jonestown for no wild Kool-Aid party," he laughed.

"Rick, I'm sorry but I have to leave," Kim said, suddenly standing and collecting her bag. "It's not you—I . . . I have to take care of something."

"What, you got to be kidding!"

"No, I'm not," she said. She bent and kissed him before dropping a fifty-dollar bill on the table and walking toward the lounge. Mojo and Kwabena were gone, and, when she stepped outside, she glanced up and down Lenox Avenue but didn't see them. A moment later, she hailed a livery cab. She called the precinct again from the car but Lt. Jackson had not returned. As the cab pulled up at 99th Street, she decided that tomorrow morning she'd call Josephine St. Claire in New Orleans. Maurice would check out Mojo and Kwabena, if she ever got in touch with him. But she had to do something. Maybe this St. Claire woman in Louisiana knew something, and perhaps, if she was into this thing as deeply as Ruff Daddy said, she could help.

ELEVEN

Warren, Ohio

Frank Napolini kissed his wife, buttoned the jacket of his navy-blue, lightweight wool suit, and stepped out onto the portico of his family's eight-bedroom mansion. The suit was custom made and imported from Italy, as were most of the mansion's finer touches, including the inlaid marble tiles on which Napolini now stood. The forty-nine-year-old underboss was a traditionalist. Family and protocol were foremost in his rigidly controlled world. That is why he had insisted on moving into the large house when his father, boss of the Napolini family, moved into a somewhat smaller, more discreet home in an exclusive, gated community in nearby Howland Township. The sprawling twenty-acre plot on which the mansion sat was his fiefdom, a tribute to the family name and a reflection of the rewards that hard work and ruthless business practices could bring. As was his custom, he scanned the manicured lawns, putting green, and Olympic-size pool, and smiled before walking over to the black Lincoln Town Car that awaited him in the circular driveway.

Alonzo Rizzo, his chauffeur, bodyguard, and long-time friend, greeted him. Rizzo, or Snake, as intimate associates called him, was a captain and the most trusted member of Napolini's crew. Rizzo and Napolini had grown up together, taken the oath, and been "straightened out" at the same time. Although he was a slight, seemingly good-humored man, and weighed only 160 pounds, Rizzo was known for his vicious temper and facility with a garrote or knife. Napolini was more imposing physically. With his heavy eyebrows and bold features, older women insisted he looked like the '60s movie star, Victor Mature. Fit, more than six feet tall, and weighing about 200 pounds, Napolini looked ten years younger than his age. Still, it was Rizzo who struck fear into those he met.

Inside the car, Napolini sat in back and lit a cigar as Rizzo guided the Lincoln out onto Hidden Lakes Drive, the semiprivate road that led to the mansion. There were two other houses on the isolated, half-mile-long road, one of them owned by a judge from nearby Youngstown who was on Napolini's payroll. Napolini smiled broadly as he passed the judge's home. Yes, this was his world, he thought. He controlled every bit of it, even the people he allowed to live on his street.

Normally, at this hour in the afternoon, Napolini would stop by the social club at the rear of his pizza parlor for a meeting with his captains and their soldiers, but today there wasn't time. He had to attend a sit-down with associates from Cleveland and Detroit at six o'clock. Louie Marino, his *consigliere*, would take care of things at the club, straighten out any difficulties, and make sure all the pickups had been made. He had other things on his mind. The most pressing of which was his nephew, Riccardo.

He had been almost a father to the kid since Johnnie, his older brother and Riccardo's father, had been dumped in McKelvey Lake ten years ago. Frank knew it could easily have been he who took the hit; in fact, he should have been the one to put some muscle on the loan shark who was siphoning off family money. His brother had agreed to do it so Frank could see his mistress that night. Frank had never forgiven himself, but he had taken care of his nephew.

The kid was ambitious, maybe overly so, Napolini thought. Riccardo had dropped out of Youngstown State University in his junior year at age twenty-one. A year later he made his first hit and got his button shortly afterward. Frank had brought him along, setting him up with a construction-union kickback scheme and a few small-time gambling operations. But Riccardo had quickly started bringing in his own deals, most recently the diamond scam. It was a money-maker and, so far, had paid big dividends. Riccardo had been made a captain on his thirtieth birthday, shortly after he sealed the deal.

But Napolini wasn't so sure it was worth all the problems—particularly after the call from Klaus Svrenson, Kees Van derVall's death, and the Las Vegas hit. All hell was breaking loose, which is why the meeting had been arranged this evening. In addition, Riccardo was getting a little too ambitious for Napolini's taste. He felt he had to talk to his nephew, set things straight, which is why he'd instructed Rizzo to stop at Joey Chaffaro's.

The small bar and Southern Italian restaurant on Route 422, the Warren-Niles Strip, was a hangout for Riccardo and his crew. When Rizzo pulled the Lincoln into the parking lot, Napolini immediately recognized Riccardo's red Porsche. Rizzo preceded him as the two men entered. As usual, at this hour the horseshoe-shaped bar in the front room was filled with a mixed crowd of retirees—locals attracted by the inexpensive food and drink—and a younger group of gamblers, wanna-bes, and connected guys. Most of them knew Napolini, and when he entered nearly all rose to pay their respects. He took a minute to move along the bar, shake hands with a few, and say hello to Rita, the cute, twenty-something bartender who smiled invitingly. Rizzo stood by the door, smiling but scrutinizing every move that was made.

A moment later Napolini strode into the Brier Hill Room to the left of the bar, where Riccardo and two of his guys were seated at a table having a late lunch.

"Uncle Frank, how are you?" Riccardo said as he quickly stood and embraced Napolini before kissing his cheek. He and Rizzo also embraced. Riccardo's companions repeated the ritual.

"Look, Rico, I need to talk to you," Napolini said as he sat down at the table. "Tell them to wait outside."

Riccardo nodded his head, and his guys left without a word. Rizzo followed them and closed the curtains at the entrance. The cute bartender brought Napolini a glass of Chianti, smiled, and left.

"So, what brings you down here to your old haunt?" Riccardo said. "You ain't been here since the old days when you and pop used to hang out."

"Yeah, the good old days, right. And you were always in here trying to sneak out with some booze or get some tail."

"Hey, the apple don't fall far from the tree, right?"

Napolini relit his cigar and leaned back in his chair, shifting to a serious expression. "So what's goin' on with this diamond thing? Any word on what really happened in Amsterdam or who put out the Las Vegas hit?"

"No . . . ah, not yet," Riccardo said, nervously fidgeting with his glass.

"I thought you were taking care of the problem."

"I'm on it, Uncle Frank, I swear. But it's difficult getting word from Europe, and, over here, everybody's clamming up. I talked to Pasaro, and he swears he had nothing to do with it. Doesn't know a thing, he says, although he thought about doing it himself." Riccardo laughed uneasily. "I'm checking on the others, Lozzi, Marintino, and Anfuso."

"Whatcha doing about replacing Van derVall, K.J. Hunter, and Woods—getting things started again?"

"I'm working on that too. Pasaro had to go to New York, but he's going to Vegas with one of our guys next week. Amsterdam will take a few more days; for now we'll work with Petris Nicholov and his contacts. Hunter's gonna be tough to replace."

Napolini tapped his cigar on the edge of the ashtray and stared up at the overhead fan, deep in thought. "There's a lot of money involved, Rico. It's a sweet deal. Nevertheless, I'm thinking about pulling out of it."

"Pulling out?"

"That's right, it's drawing too much attention to us. Too many guys have been whacked. Sooner or later the Feds are gonna trace it back to us. Now we got people inside the organization turning on each other, families pointing the finger at one another, and too many people we don't control are involved. It's beginning to smell. I don't trust the fucking foreigners — that English prick would turn his shorts around in a minute. And forget about the Africans and these damn performers, especially the rappers! They're fucking crazy."

"Yeah, but with the rocks they usually wear and the attitude they got, nobody's better at walking through customs without being checked. There's no better cover for getting diamonds back into the country. Look, Uncle Frank, the deal is worth millions to us, as much as we're taking in from most of our other operations combined. We can't just stick to the old ways. We gotta keep up with the times. You can't pull out!"

"Yeah, I can," Napolini said calmly. "I don't like Klaus, but he warned us that this thing could blow up in our faces. I'm not risking everything we've worked for on something this shaky. Clean it up, quick, or ditch it. Is that clear?"

Napolini stood up and finished his wine as Riccardo stared at him in disbelief. "*Ciao,*" the older man said, "call me tomorrow. I'm bringing this up at the meeting this evening. I'll let you know what the others think."

Riccardo stood and hugged him before he left.

Rizzo remained at the door watching the two soldiers who sat slumped on bar stools as Napolini left the restaurant. When Riccardo joined them, Rizzo turned and left. No one said a word.

Rizzo parked the Lincoln Town Car at five-thirty near the large red canopy in front of Alberini's restaurant. The traditional eatery with its old-world decor had been one of the premier Italian restaurants in the area for decades. It also boasted "one of the world's best wine cellars," which is why Napolini had made it one of his favorites. He and Rizzo walked past the glass-enclosed solarium and main dining room with its floor-to-ceiling mural of Venice; up the stairs they passed the private dining room that was being set up for the meeting and entered the dimmed bar and lounge with its stained-glass windows and Tiffany lamps. Napolini ordered a bottle of 1997 Estancia Meritage and Rizzo a beer as they settled in to wait for the others to arrive. Fifteen minutes later, Louie Marino joined them. He was the family's most trusted advisor; both Frank Napolini and his father, the family boss, relied on his counsel.

"How'd things go at the club?" Napolini asked.

"No problems," Marino said as he took a seat at the bar. The bartender poured a glass of wine for the bespectacled *consigliere*.

"What do you think, Louie," Napolini said, "should we dump this diamond shit? It's gettin' too fucking messy."

"Hard to balance the potential profit against the risks, but I lean toward movin' away from it," Marino said, "especially with all the crap goin' on here now. It's already too hot. I helped your pop set up the business, you know that, and to tell you the truth, I don't trust this thing. We don't control enough of the shit, too many loose cannons, you know what I mean? I don't want to see you get involved in something that'll bring us down, Frank."

"Yeah, that's how I feel, but what about Riccardo? The kid's got his heart set on this deal."

"Hey," Marino laughed, "you know how it is with these young Turks—got more balls than brains. It looked like a winner, no doubt. But you got to be wise enough to know when to step back."

Rizzo leaned over and whispered to Napolini, "I think they're set, Frank. Ignazio's signaling from the doorway."

Napolini and Marino rose and started for the entrance to the private dining room at the center of the restaurant. "Don't worry, the kid'll get over it," Marino said as they entered.

"The only thing I'm concerned with right now is how the *ossobuco alla milanese* is tonight," Napolini laughed.

"Ah . . . and the *tagliatelle al pesto*," Marino offered.

Inside the walnut-paneled room, they greeted the eight men who had arrived from Cleveland and Detroit. They were seated around a long mahogany table in tufted leather Chippendale chairs; a crystal chandelier hung overhead. When the curtains were drawn across the floor-to-ceiling windows at the entranceway, Rizzo, arms folded, took a position outside the door with Ignazio, one of the Cleveland guests' bodyguards.

It was nearly two hours later when the ten men emerged smiling from the room. They shook hands, hugged, and then, in small groups, straggled out of the restaurant, which was now packed with Sunday evening dinner guests. Outside, Napolini asked Marino to join him in the Lincoln, Rizzo would bring him back to pick up his car later, he told him. In the backseat of the car, the two men discussed the meeting as Rizzo cruised along the back roads that fed into the Strip, stopping occasionally to attend to family business.

"The kid's gonna be fucked up when he hears what we decided," Napolini said as they sat in the parking lot of Opus Twenty One, the trendy restaurant at Avalon Lakes Golf Course. Napolini had sent Rizzo in to tell Lillian, a twenty-two-year-old waitress and his latest outside diversion, that he would pick her up at 9:30.

"Not to worry," Marino said, "Rico's got to learn that the organization comes first. Anyway, we're givin' him two weeks to straighten this shit out."

"Yeah, but you know I hate to turn him down after what happened to Johnnie. He still doesn't know what really happened that night, does he?"

"No, not as far as I know. But you gotta stop blaming yourself for that—who knew that asshole would flip out and fire on Johnnie. Nobody else knows what happened but me and your father, the don, and neither one of us is gonna say a word."

"Well, you never know when one of the shark's buddies will step up and drop a dime, try to split up the organization. Anyway, he can be a hothead, and this deal was his baby. We'll have to watch him for a while, in case he can't make it right."

"He's a smart kid, Frank, he won't fuck up now," Marino laughed and patted his friend on the knee. "We ain't gonna be here forever, you know. He'll be running things himself soon enough."

When Rizzo returned to the car, Napolini told him to stop by the Crown Hill Burial Park. The small cemetery was just north of Route 422 on Franklin Street. Despite his sometimes brutal line of work, Napolini considered himself a devout man, and he appreciated quiet and solitude. He often stopped at Crown Hill to meditate and think, or, as was the case today, to speak confidentially to a close associate or friend. When Rizzo parked, Napolini and Marino strolled over to the rectangular marble monument and benches placed near the center of the grounds. Rizzo stayed behind, leaning on the Town Car and watching the entrance to make sure that no other automobiles entered the deserted cemetery. From his vantage point he could see the two men clearly even though it was twilight and they were about a hundred yards away.

Napolini and Marino lit cigars and, seated on one of the marble benches, admired the detailed rendering of the Last Supper that had been etched on the monument. It was a perfect place to relax, and the men continued their conversation as the sun slowly dipped below the horizon. Neither of them saw the two figures in stocking masks who silently crept up behind the Lincoln and clubbed Rizzo on the head. A few minutes later, after crouching and skulking from one gravestone to another, they lay ten feet behind their targets. In unison they rose and aimed shotguns at the backs of the two men on the marble bench. They fired simultaneously and, as the sound of the blasts broke the silence and echoed through the cemetery, Napolini and Marino slumped to the grass. The shooters sprinted back past the Town Car and the still unconscious Rizzo, then down the hill where they disappeared into the darkness.

Freetown

Ezekiel Kwabena relaxed in the backseat of the Mercedes as it slowly wound its way toward Freetown. He had departed New York's Kennedy Airport at 6:00 A.M. on Thursday for the long flight back to Sierra Leone. Seven hours later he arrived at Brussels International Airport, where there was a two-hour layover. As usual, he had switched briefcases with a Belgian contact inside the VIP passenger lounge. When he boarded the six-hour flight to Liberia's Monrovia Payne Airport, he was carrying more than $500,000 in cash. From Monrovia he took a small private plane and arrived at Lungi International Airport in Sierra Leone at about 1:45 A.M. West African time. He was met by his driver and an armed bodyguard, who now accompanied him on the almost one-hour drive to Freetown.

Kwabena placed his hand on the revolver that the bodyguard had given him at the airport and pulled the leather briefcase closer to his side as the car cruised through the moonlit countryside along the partially paved Peninsula Highway. Although he had taken the route hundreds of times, this part of the trip was always a little harrowing. Heavily armed government troops manned the roads and there were frequent stops and checkpoints, but there was still the real possibility of attack by members of the Revolutionary United Front.

Staring out at the hypnotic dance of headlights on the darkened road, Kwabena tried to relax. And within moments, as he thought about the last few years, a smile came to his face. Yes, he had come a long way: four years ago, he'd been just an anonymous clerk in the government Gold and Diamond Office who lived in near poverty at Bo. But he had attracted the attention of his superiors when he devised several efficient and practical ways of facilitating the diamond mining process while eliminating some of the inevitable theft associated with it. He was promoted and moved to the central mining office in Freetown a year later. There he quickly established associations with high-ranking government officials, and demonstrated that his negotiating skills were as advanced as his administrative ones. "Ambassador" was an honorific he acquired by achievement, not by appointment.

When he was given the opportunity to travel to Europe and the United States as a liaison between the government and diamond conglomerates like De Beers, his talents became more evident and eventually essential. He had quickly risen to the top of his agency and established himself as the key figure in Sierra Leone's diamond export trade. He'd worked diligently for his country, but he had also served his own interests. And when he was approached by Klaus Svrenson, whom he met at a convention in Antwerp, Kwabena had not declined the Swede's offer to "discuss" an alternative method of redirecting some of his country's resources to benefit himself. He was aware of the criminal involvement of the mob in America and the thin line he straddled with regard to so-called conflict diamonds. But, except for Clarence Johnson, he didn't see or deal with the unsavory elements involved in the deal. He worked with businessmen and politicians like the late Dave Hamlin. Now, however, the riffraff was rising to the top, and his position was being compromised and threatened. Fortunately, he had been preparing for just such a disaster. In a matter of months, he would leave the whole business behind him.

He breathed a sigh of relief when the car reached Freetown and began the ascent to Juba, the exclusive hillside area in which he and many middle-class, professional and government-connected residents lived. As the Mercedes wound its way up the steep, circuitous road, Kwabena gazed down at the central city and seaport. The city was under curfew and at this hour there was little activity, only pockets of lights were to be seen at Lagoonda, the casino hotel, and a few other tourist spots.

Shortly after passing Kabassa Lodge, the huge compound that had been the residence of several former presidents, the driver stopped and stepped out of the car to speak to one of the armed troops stationed at the gate leading to Kwabena's housing complex. When one of the soldiers, a round-faced youth of only seventeen, recognized Kwabena, he waved the car through. A few minutes later, a guard opened the security gate leading to the grounds of Kwabena's large Moroccan-style stone home.

The driver left after two servants rushed outside to retrieve the luggage, but the bodyguard accompanied Kwabena into the house and stationed himself in the foyer, a few steps from the huge oak front door. Kwabena passed a second guard and two Dobermans sitting at the bottom of the stairs and staring at the door. Still clutching the briefcase, he went upstairs. He first looked in on his two children, who were sound asleep in their own bedrooms. After checking on his wife, who was also asleep, and placing his revolver on the bedside table, he went to his study. He dismissed the young female servant who had been following him, waiting for instructions, by telling her he wouldn't need anything further this evening.

Inside the study, he locked the door and went to his safe, which was concealed in the bottom of the pedestal on which an eighteenth-century, Mendes figure was displayed. Kwabena carefully unpacked the stacks of crisp one-hundred-dollar bills and placed them with the uncut diamonds and the pile of money already in the safe. When he finished, he stood and stared out of the window at the few lights still flickering in the troubled city below. He was almost there, he thought; two, maybe three more trips, and he could quit and move to the Caribbean home that he had purchased last year. It was far too dangerous, and becoming increasingly more treacherous each day.

He turned out the lights, stepped outside the study, and locked the door. Before entering the bathroom to prepare for bed, he looked over the balcony to reassure himself that both the guard stationed at the front door and the heavily armed soldier at the bottom of the stairs were still there. Satisfied, he walked into the bathroom, flicked on the light, and bent over the sink. There was a slight rustling of the shower curtain before the light suddenly went out again, and, as he turned toward the switch, he felt a hemp cord graze the top of his forehead before it was yanked down to his neck. He struggled and tried to scream, but the thick rough fiber had not only cut off the air leading to his lungs but also stifled his vocal cords. All he could do was tug at the rope and gasp. A moment or so later, Kwabena sank to the floor clutching the cord in a dead-man's grip.

TWELVE

New Orleans — Friday, August 3

Kim Carlyle's plane touched down at New Orleans International Airport shortly before noon. As she made her way through the terminal, she had to stop herself from pushing past the lines of people leisurely sauntering down the long gray halls toward the baggage claim area. She was impatient; there was no time to waste.

She wove through the crowd, speeding past a slender Asian man walking a few paces ahead of her and practically knocking over an elderly couple when the woman stopped short to adjust the strap on her shoulder bag. The old man yelled something surprisingly obscene at Kim's back. She mumbled a halfhearted apology over her shoulder but never slowed down as she dashed through the wide glass doors, hailed a cab, and headed toward the heart of the French Quarter.

As her cab moved along in traffic, Kim thought back to the call that she'd received from Josephine St. Claire. Kim had tried calling her several times the day before, but there was no answer. She had left two messages and spent the day doing some research on the woman. Finally, earlier this morning, St. Claire had returned her call, and she sounded desperate. Kim wasn't sure why she had called at six o'clock that morning, but she was convinced that St. Claire was in serious trouble.

St. Claire was an international art dealer known in celebrity jet-set circles for her exquisite beauty and poise. She'd been born into an old-money, mulatto family that had been seated at the pinnacle of colored society in New Orleans since the eighteenth century. She could trace her ancestry back to some of the greatest houses in Holland, France, and Spain. Her great-, great-, great-grandmother had been an intimate of Marie Lavaux, the legendary voodoo queen. Since that time, there were persistent rumors that the family's wealth and good fortune, including the lavish home that her grandfather had left her, stemmed not from hard work or even luck, but other, more sinister forces.

The cab stopped at the corner of Prytania and Third Streets in front of a colossal, pre–Civil War plantation-style mansion in the middle of the Garden District. Elegant mahogany shutters sealed off a view of the inside from the street. The broad, wrap-around porch burst with potted scarlet and ginger orchids, crepe myrtle, and creeping ivy. Sweet-smelling magnolia and oleander trees shaded the three-story house on all sides. It was breathtaking. Kim could scarcely believe that a trendy twenty-eight-year-old jet-setter like St. Claire lived alone in this huge house.

She let herself in the gate, walked along the garden path lined with yellow rosebushes, and went up the short flight of steps to the front porch. Kim rang the bell and waited. No answer. She rang again and looked around for any sign of life within the mansion. Nothing.

She was rooting through her purse for her cellphone so that she could call inside when the door finally creaked open. Josephine St.

Claire was hiding behind the door. She peeked out just far enough to grab Kim's arm and practically yanked her in off the porch.

The house was as dark as night inside. As Kim's eyes adjusted to the abrupt shift, she heard St. Claire behind her locking the three dead bolts on the door and pulling the chain back through its eye.

"Come this way," St. Claire whispered. She took Kim's hand and led her through the wide hallway until they came to a steep flight of stairs. Without flicking on the light, she walked down the stairs and waited at the landing for Kim to follow. Kim was reluctant to descend the darkened stairs. She didn't want to trip and fall. More important, she wanted to know exactly what was waiting for her at the bottom.

"Turn on the light," Kim called.

"No," St. Claire answered. "Not until we get into the sanctuary room. I don't want to take a chance on anyone seeing where we've gone."

"But we're the only ones here."

"Maybe."

Every bit of training that Kim had ever received in the department cried out in protest against this scenario. This was absolutely crazy. But for some reason, Kim's instincts told her to go along with it. For now.

She held on to the banister with one hand and, with her other hand pressed against the wall, guided herself down the stairs. Even though she was wearing soft tennis shoes that made no noise, the weight of her body caused the wood stairs to creak loudly underneath her. At the landing, St. Claire grabbed her hand and led her into a room on the right.

She closed and locked the door behind them. Then she turned on the light. Kim had to cover her eyes with her hand for a minute because of the glare. Then, slowly, she began to look around.

The room was white. Even the smooth concrete floor, which had a drain in the center, was white. An altar covered in dead flowers with a picture of two serpents intertwined stood directly ahead of them. On the floor in front of the altar Kim saw three bowls filled with water, rosary beads, some sort of grayish meat on a plate, and about a dozen pennies strewn among the objects. Tall white candles surrounded the altar and were placed in the corners of the room. Lining the wall to the left was a long cabinet filled with jars and bottles. On the right was a sink with a hose attachment to the faucet. The room smelled of frankincense, spoiled meat, and melted candle wax.

"What is this place?" Kim asked.

"It's my sanctuary," St. Claire replied. "No one else has a key. It's the only place that I feel safe anymore."

For the first time, Kim turned to face St. Claire in full light. What she saw made her gasp softly.

St. Claire looked haggard. Her smooth, almond complexion had turned to an uneven, pasty yellow. She had bags under her eyes and she had broken out with fiery red pimples across her forehead and cheeks. Even her thick, luxurious auburn hair, which she generally wore loose and swinging almost to her waist, seemed dry and brittle. She had it pulled back into a tight braid, and the style made her face look even more severe. Kim couldn't be sure, but St. Claire appeared much thinner than in the pictures Kim had seen.

"What's going on?" Kim asked softly. "What's this all about? Why did you call me here?"

"Well," St. Claire answered, "I—I'm afraid. I think someone's trying to kill me."

"Why? Who would want to kill you?"

"I'm pretty sure it's that gangster from Ohio. I don't know if you've heard of him, but his name is Frank Napolini, and I think he's after me because I have this."

St. Claire walked over to the altar and removed the picture of the snakes, which she gently placed on the floor. There was a safe behind the picture, and she opened it without even attempting to make sure that Kim wasn't checking out the combination. She pulled out a black satin bag and closed the safe. Then she sat down on the floor, opened the bag, and took out a black velvet cloth, which she placed on the floor in front of her. St. Claire motioned to Kim to sit opposite her.

"So what's in the bag?" Kim asked, even though she was almost certain that she already knew.

St. Claire turned the bag over and emptied out its contents onto the cloth on the floor. Diamonds spilled out over the velvet, glittering and rolling so close to Kim's crossed legs that she could have reached out and grabbed a handful. But she didn't move. Instead, she sat silently and waited for St. Claire to explain what was going on.

St. Claire held one of the diamonds up toward the light.

"This is a class D, a River diamond. It's absolutely flawless. Just about the best quality you can get. You see the shape? It's a round brilliant-cut stone. This one little diamond right here is only about three and a half carats. Not even the size of my pinky nail. And yet, it's worth about $90,000."

Kim quickly scanned the diamonds on the cloth in front of her. There was a mound of about forty or fifty of them.

"Yes. You're looking at more than four million dollars. Hard to believe, isn't it?"

"So, you stole these from Napolini?"

"No, I didn't. They came to me through . . . someone else."

"Who?"

"Well—"

"Look," Kim said, "this is no time for games. If your life is in danger, and I believe it is, then mine is also. I'm sitting here with you watching you play with a lapful of stolen diamonds worth millions. If you can't be straight with me, I'm leaving."

"It's not that I don't want to tell you," St. Claire rushed to explain; "it's just that I'm afraid. Someone broke into my house yesterday. I'm sure it wasn't just a random burglary. I'd seen that man recently in Europe, which leads me to believe that he'd been watching me for a long time. I was walking home at about three in the morning, and I saw him sneak into the gate and go around the back of the house. I followed him back there and saw that he'd broken in through a back window and disabled my alarm system. That terrified me. He had to be a professional. I have an extremely high-tech alarm system that's monitored directly by the New Orleans police department. So either he knew how to disable it or he had help getting in. There was no way I was going to confront him. And I was too afraid to call the police because they'd start asking questions that I couldn't answer. So I waited.

"My car was parked around the corner, and I stayed in it all night," she continued. "At dawn, I got up the courage to go inside and I found the house empty. That's when I got your messages. At first I thought that he must've gone out through another window. But all of the other windows and doors were still locked from the inside. Then I realized that the door leading down to the sanctuary was open. I came down here and looked around, but nothing was wrong. This inner door was still locked, too.

"When I went back upstairs, I noticed that there were three large splatters of blood by the front door. That was the only indication I found of someone being in the house. Of course, my question was how did the blood get there and what happened to the man? Was someone else in the house waiting for me when the other guy snuck in? That's what I think. I also think that if I hadn't seen that man come in here and stayed away last night, I'd be dead already."

"You still haven't answered my question," Kim persisted. "Where did you get the diamonds?"

Finally St. Claire relented. "Some were shipped directly to me. They came with the artwork. And some, well . . . they came from Clarence . . . most people call him Mojo."

"Clarence Johnson, from New York?"

"Yes."

"I've heard of him. Ruff Daddy told—"

"Ruff Daddy? Where is he? Is he all right?"

"Yes, I think so. But he's also running scared. He's hiding out some-where. When he called, he told me to contact you," Kim said. "But how do you know Mojo?"

"He's my spiritual advisor. The leader of our religion."

Kim noted that St. Claire had said "our" religion and that she seemed to be taking it all very, very seriously.

"So where did Mojo get the diamonds?"

"There were a number of ways. I'm not sure about all of them, but I think it all leads back to Klaus Svrenson and Frank Napolini. Mojo was never very open about his contacts and exactly how everything worked. He told me about a year ago that he'd had a way to make a lot of money fast. He was set to buy a large piece of property down in the Islands. He wanted to build a school and a compound there to house and train priests and priestesses. It's been his dream for most of his life. He'd do just about anything to realize it. I, obviously, never needed the money. But I had all the means and connections that Mojo needed, so I said I'd help in any way I could.

"It was all supposed to be so simple. But something else is going on here. Somebody changed the rules. I don't know how and I don't know why. I know they want the diamonds back but I don't think that's all of it. If it was, I'd just try to call Napolini or Svrenson and tell them to call off the dogs and I'd return the diamonds. That's why, when I got your message, I called in the middle of the night. I knew that you had been concerned about this since the beginning, when Tiffany died. And if anyone could help, you would."

"I'll try to get to the bottom of this, Josephine. You know I will. I have some ideas, but nothing solid yet. Ruff Daddy said you might have some information."

"Anything I can do to help you, I'll do it."

"Tell me where Klaus is."

St. Claire hesitated.

"Hey, you just told me you'd do everything you could. Now you won't even answer a simple question. Give me something, Josephine. Did it ever occur to you that Klaus or even Mojo might be the one that's after you?"

"Oh no!" St. Claire shook her head. "Mojo would never have anything to do with this."

"How do you know that?"

St. Claire got up and walked over to the cabinet against the wall. She pulled out a small glass bottle with a plastic stopper in the top, came back over, and showed it to Kim.

"What is this?" Kim asked.

"It's angleworm dust mixed with High John the Conqueror root."

"What does it do?"

"You drink it and it puts love in your heart."

"Girl, are you crazy? You think because you poured some magic potion in his milk one night, he's head over heels in love with you?"

St. Claire nodded, suddenly looking very childish and naive—nothing like the sophisticated, worldly woman Kim had expected to meet.

"What makes you think it really worked?"

"I know it did!" St. Claire answered defensively.

"Okay, so maybe it's not Mojo. But what about Klaus, and, tell me, exactly how did you help Mojo get the diamonds?"

Just then the women heard a loud crash above their heads. St. Claire leapt to her feet and backed up against the wall. Kim quickly scooped up the diamonds and put them back into the bag, which she tossed over by the altar. Then she switched off the overhead light and ran to the door. She felt through the dark for the lock on the door and unlocked it.

"No, no—come back," St. Claire whispered. "What are you doing?"

"Shhh!" Kim listened for the creak of the stairs. Silence. No one was coming down—not yet.

"Come on. Let's go."

Kim could hear St. Claire whimpering in the dark, on the verge of tears.

"Josephine, if we stay down here, we'll be trapped like cornered animals. If we can get upstairs, we might be able to get out of the house without being seen. At the very least, we'll have a chance to fight. Now let's go!"

Kim started out the door and up the stairs. St. Claire quieted down and, almost instantly, was at her side. She didn't want to be left behind. They crept slowly up the stairs, freezing each time the stairs squeaked. For the first time in years, Kim wished she had her service revolver. As it was, she had nothing with which to defend herself, not even a can of Mace.

When they reached the top of the stairs, Kim slowly opened the door. She heard a noise that sounded like it was coming from their left. Kim looked down the long, dim hall to the left then to the right. She didn't see anyone. Motioning for St. Claire to stay right behind her, Kim moved quickly toward the front door, keeping low and hugging the wall.

The hallway in front of them opened up into a wide foyer. The living room was off to the right, and the door to the left led to the first of two formal dining rooms. Kim hurried past the two doors toward the foyer. When they got to the front door, someone grabbed St. Claire from behind and clamped a hand over her mouth just as she started to scream. Kim whirled around and lunged at the shadowy figure, grabbing the attacker by the neck in a choke hold. Fighting against the weight of two women, the intruder pushed Kim back, banging her head into the oak-paneled wall.

Dazed and sprawled against the wall, Kim peered at her attacker's flattened features beneath the skin-tight stocking mask, before she felt a forearm slam into her stomach. She crumpled to the ground and, gagging from the force of the blow, nearly threw up.

The intruder was very strong, but not much taller or heavier than either of the two women. Kim watched in helpless panic as the attacker turned to St. Claire, grabbed her neck, and began choking her again.

Another crash upstairs startled both Kim and the intruder, who immediately released St. Claire's neck and stared toward the top of the stairs. Kim knew that if she didn't do something in that instant both she and St. Claire would be dead. Ignoring the pain that threatened to double her over, she stumbled to her feet and snatched a lamp from the table by the door. The intruder turned around just in time to throw up a hand and partially deflect the blow as Kim brought the lamp crashing down onto the top of the bobbing, masked head. The intruder sank to the floor, then collapsed in a heap. Kim stepped over the body and rushed to St. Claire.

She was coughing and dazed, but luckily she was still strong enough to walk. Kim helped her toward the door. On the way out, she grabbed a set of car keys from the table where she'd picked up the lamp. She began to fumble with the dead bolts but found, to her surprise, that they were already unlocked. Throwing open the door, Kim half-dragged, half-carried St. Claire out into the sunlight.

"Where's your car?" Kim panted.

St. Claire couldn't answer. So she pointed toward a silver convertible Mercedes parked just outside the gate at the corner. The two women struggled toward the street. Kim knew that if they could just make it out of the garden, they would have a chance. Being in the garden was almost as dangerous as being inside the house. She realized that the shady trees and dense foliage that had seemed so beautiful when she'd first looked up at the house were now the perfect cover to shield their attacker from prying eyes.

Kim heard someone moving inside the house. But she didn't turn around. They were just a few feet from the gate. They could make it.

She unlatched the gate and threw it open in one move. In seconds they were at the car. She unlocked the door, shoved St. Claire in, and closed the door behind her. Then she ran around to the driver's side and jumped in. Only after she put the key in the ignition and gunned the engine did Kim look back toward the house. She thought she glimpsed a towering man move past the still-opened front door.

That was all she needed to see. Kim gunned the engine and took off up Prytania, turned onto Camp Street, and headed toward the Quarter.

When St. Claire was finally able to catch her breath, she told Kim, "Go up Chartres Street until you get to St. Louis and make a left."

They made the left and traveled for three more blocks before St. Claire said, "Pull over."

Kim parked the car, and the two women waited. About twenty minutes later, a man turned the corner and walked into a salmon-colored townhouse.

"It's him," St. Claire said frantically.

Kim turned and saw the man enter the building. It was Mojo. He was wearing a T-shirt and jeans and had a knapsack on his back. About fifteen minutes later, he came out of the building and turned left toward Burgundy Street. The knapsack was still slung on his back, but he had changed clothes. He now wore a brown jogging suit.

Kim and St. Claire followed at a distance as he walked west. After about four more blocks, they saw him head into the St. Louis Cemetery #1.

They entered the walled cemetery just in time to see Mojo disappear behind a row of 250-year-old above-ground tombs. At the rear of the cemetery, he stopped near one of the newer tombs and looked around. Satisfied that no one was watching, he removed a slab of slate from the back of the tomb and reached inside. St. Claire let out a startled cry of disbelief. It was clear that if this had been part of any plan they had, she didn't know about it.

Kim couldn't see exactly what Mojo was doing behind the tomb, and she was anxious to get closer. But after what had just happened to them, she didn't dare. Mojo was obviously desperate if he was willing to go to one of the most popular cemeteries in New Orleans in the middle of the day and desecrate one of the tombs.

After rooting around deep inside the tomb for a minute or two, Mojo seemed to find what he was looking for. He glanced around again quickly and then stuffed a large, dark bag into his leather knapsack. He straightened up, peered down the row for the third time, then rushed toward the entrance of the cemetery. As soon as he'd rounded the corner, Kim and St. Claire dashed over to the tomb. Lester Bennett's name was engraved on the stone.

It took both women heaving with all their might to remove the slab of slate that served as a false back to the top level of the tomb. When they moved the slab, a putrid stench rushed out of the tomb so strong and fast that St. Claire doubled over and nearly vomited. Covering her mouth and nose with her hand, Kim looked inside. The coffin had been opened, but she didn't bother to look into it.

"He got the rest of the diamonds," St. Claire mumbled as Kim stepped away from the tomb.

The women replaced the slab and ran back to the entrance of the cemetery. They were hoping to catch at least a glimpse of Mojo as he made his way down Conti or St. Louis. They didn't want to lose him in the crowd. Kim thought that she saw him heading around the bend on Basin Street where it turned into Toulouse. She ran into the middle of the road, and St. Claire followed her.

"Is that him?" Kim asked.

"Yes. It is. I'm sure of it. We should—"

But St. Claire never got to finish her sentence. Kim heard the squeal of the car tires and turned her head just in time to see a small, blue Mazda barreling down on them. Behind the wheel and tinted windshield, she could make out the silhouette of someone with long flowing hair. She reached for St. Claire, but they were too far apart.

"Watch out!" Kim screamed; there was no time to move.

St. Claire turned just as the car careered into her, flipping her over the hood before it roared down Basin Street.

Kim leapt backward, flinging herself against the passenger-side door of an SUV parked behind her, and accidentally slammed her head into the window of the truck. The Mazda missed hitting her by less than a foot.

A screaming crowd raced toward St. Claire's twisted body, and a few pedestrians ran down the block to the police station at the corner.

Kim's head exploded with pain. She sank to her knees in the street as blood from the gash on the back of her skull ran down her neck. Suddenly there was a crowd standing above her, people telling her to lie still, help was coming. She tried to get up and go see about St. Claire, but someone restrained her. She struggled to keep her head clear, but she felt as though she was drifting in the middle of a dream, a terrible nightmare from which she couldn't escape.

Moments later, a uniformed policewoman kneeled next to her, checking her pulse and asking if she was okay. The blare of an approaching ambulance siren roared in the background, and Kim could barely hear the officer above the noise. Everything seemed distant and blurry as she felt herself being lifted onto a gurney and rolled toward the ambulance.

THIRTEEN

NEW ORLEANS/NEW YORK—SATURDAY, AUGUST 4

New Orleans

When Kim awoke at 11 A.M., she was lying in a bed in the Tulane University Hospital and Clinic. The other bed in the double room was empty. A light gauze bandage was wrapped around her head. Except for a slight headache there were no other signs of injury, and aside from a little drowsiness, she felt fine. She had awakened several times during the night, and she knew that at some point doctors had given her a sedative. Now she eased herself up to a sitting position and pressed the bedside button to signal a nurse. When a bouncy young RN appeared, she informed Kim that she had suffered only a mild concussion and would be back on her feet in a day or so. After routine temperature and blood pressure tests, she turned to leave.

"The doctor will be in to see you in minute," she said. "And, oh, the police want to talk to you also. There's a detective waiting downstairs."

Suddenly the events of the past day began flashing through her mind—the intruder, the diamonds, Mojo, then the Mazda speeding toward them. But what had happened to St. Claire? Did she survive, and, if so, where was she?

The doctor arrived first and confirmed that her injury was not serious; however, as a precaution, he wanted to keep her at the hospital for observation until the next day. He also told her that St. Claire had died en route to the hospital and offered his condolences before leaving.

The hard-nosed Cajun detective who entered a moment later was not nearly as amenable. Detective Louis Benoit questioned Kim for more than a half hour about the hit-and-run killing, insisting that she must have known the driver because witnesses said the car appeared to be pursuing her and St. Claire. Kim had no intention of revealing anything about Mojo, the diamonds, or the events preceding the attack to the New Orleans police force before she had time to think about it. So she steadfastly insisted that she didn't know the driver, which was not a lie. She did provide as detailed a description of the assailant as she could, pointing out that all she had seen before she blacked out was the silhouette of a figure with long hair behind the tinted windshield.

Annoyed with her unwillingness to provide any information about why she had come to New Orleans to see Josephine St. Claire and what had precipitated the attack, Benoit finally threatened to hold Kim as a material witness to the murder. When she revealed that she was a former New York police officer, however, he backed down. "Don't leave New Orleans without informing us," he said before stomping out.

When he left, Kim immediately tried dialing Lt. Jackson in New York to report what had happened the previous day. She couldn't reach him, and, when lunch arrived a few minutes later, she realized she hadn't eaten in twenty-four hours. She was famished. She settled back in bed and eagerly devoured the plain, institutional meal. Shortly after the tray was removed, the bedside telephone rang.

"Hello?" she said in a questioning tone, surprised that anyone knew where she was.

"Hallo, Kim," the singsong Swedish voice replied.

"Klaus? Klaus Svrenson . . . where are you? And how . . . how did you know I was here?"

"It didn't take a genius, my friend. You've been all over the local news, and, well, did you think Josephine was working alone? Of course, I knew."

Kim paused, noting that he said local news, which suggested he was somewhere in the area. "Right, right," she said, "but where have you been? You know that everyone, including the police, is out looking for you."

"I am aware of that, but, like our friend Ruff Daddy, I'm not anxious to be seen right now. I know all this looks bad for me, but believe it or not, I'm as frightened by these events as Ruff Daddy. I called because I'd like to know if you've discovered anything that might help me find out who's killing these people. I need to protect myself. Frankly, Kim, I'm scared."

"What? You're scared!"

"Of course! That's why I need to know who you saw at Josephine's house yesterday. You're the only one still living who's seen the killer. What happened there? Who was it?"

"Wait . . . wait a minute. How did you know I was at Josephine's home. That couldn't have been on the news since I didn't tell anyone and Josephine is dead."

"As I said, Josephine was not working alone. I know exactly what time you arrived at her house. What I don't know is what happened inside. Who did you see? That's the person we should both be looking for."

Kim hesitated. She didn't trust Klaus and wasn't sure of his motives. But he obviously knew that she and Josephine had met and then escaped from the house with someone in pursuit. She was sure that he wasn't the intruder, the person had been much smaller and far too short. But it might have been someone he sent. Klaus could just be digging for information to determine if she could identify an intruder who might later identify him.

"Look, Kim, the killer knows who you are now. You're no safer than I am. Tell me what you know."

"First, tell me something. Was it you who set up this whole diamond-smuggling operation, recruiting people from Europe and Africa? How big is it, Klaus? And how could you involve your own wife?"

"You don't know what you're talking about, Kim. But that's not the point now. And, if I did, do you really think I'd talk about it on this phone with that nosy detective lurking around the hospital? It's time to stop playing at being a cop. It's foolish. Tell me what you know, and maybe I can help prevent your being hurt."

"Why don't you meet me, Klaus, let's talk about this. I can help you if you're involved."

"I can only tell you that, after Tiffany's death, I may have unwittingly set all of this in motion. Some of my associates, it seems, are more brutal than I suspected."

"What are you sa—"

"Enough, Kim! I don't have time for this! And neither do you. If you won't cooperate, I can't protect you. You're on your own."

Before Kim could respond, Klaus hung up.

Frustrated, Kim slammed the receiver down and sat up in bed. She wasn't sure whether to believe Klaus or not. But if he had found her in the hospital, then the hit-and-run driver could easily do the same thing. Klaus was right about one thing though, she was in danger—from the intruder or maybe even from Klaus. She wasn't safe in the hospital.

She got up and, on wobbly legs, went to the closet to check for her clothes. Within a half hour she had dressed and slipped out of the hospital. She walked a few blocks before hailing a cab. After stopping at a cut-rate drugstore in the Quarter, where she bought sunglasses and a cheap Afro wig, she continued to the airport. It was after two o'clock when she bought a ticket to New York. While waiting for the plane to depart, she called Lt. Jackson and, this time, got through to him.

Lt. Jackson was silent as she related in detail everything that happened in New Orleans, including the call from Klaus. When she finished he told her that they had put Kwabena and Mojo under surveillance, but both of them had left New York on Thursday. Since they had no real evidence, neither could be detained. Neither had returned to his knowledge. He would, however, immediately order someone to watch Mojo's house and store this afternoon.

"What about you," he said finally, "are you going to be all right?"

"Yes," Kim said. "No one will ever recognize me in this tacky outfit. I'm taking a four-thirty flight to LaGuardia. I'll call when I arrive at my apartment."

"Fine, but I'm going to station someone outside, just in case. They'll be waiting when you arrive at your place."

"Thanks, Maurice," Kim laughed. "I knew that deep down you always loved me."

"Yeah, right. I'll talk to you when you get here."

New York

Mojo carefully pulled the curtain away from the side of the window, leaving a half-inch opening. He stooped and peeked through the slit. The unmarked police car was still parked across the street from the Old World Music Shop. Mojo stepped away from the window and moved to the rear of the darkened store. Passing through the office, he went to the windowless back room; the lone overhead light was turned on. Mojo sat on the floor next to a large attaché case that he had packed when he cleaned out the safe, then checked his watch. It was 8:45 P.M. Another hour and he'd be on his way.

He had arrived in New York earlier that morning, after flying in from New Orleans. Avoiding his Lenox Terrace apartment, he went directly to the record store. No one had been watching the shop, but he entered through the rear, leaving the front door padlocked from the outside and making sure to keep the lights off. He slept in the office. It was during those hours of restless sleep that he determined to get out immediately.

He had gone to New Orleans to see Josephine St. Claire and get the diamonds from her and from Lester's grave. When he found the Hispanic burglar rummaging through St. Claire's things, he'd been forced to kill him. No one was going to take what he had worked so hard to accumulate. That's when he decided he'd have to leave Josephine behind. Someone was on to her, and he couldn't afford to let anybody else discover that they worked together. He hid the Hispanic man's body in the attic, but before he could go back to get the diamonds, Josephine returned. Then the other woman arrived.

He was waiting for the opportunity to snatch the diamonds when the second intruder arrived. He had watched the struggle in the foyer from the second-floor balcony, and, if the other woman hadn't hit the attacker with a lamp, he would have intervened. But it had worked out perfectly. When the women left, the intruder was unconscious and Mojo took the opportunity to retrieve the diamonds from the sanctuary. As far as he knew, he had escaped without being noticed. After a quick trip to the cemetery, he had gone to the airport.

Now he sat waiting for Shawayne, one of his first recruits, to come and drive him to the airport. He had called Shawayne when he noticed the police car outside the record shop earlier that afternoon. He instructed the eager young disciple to bring him a change of clothes, park the car around the corner on 119th Street, and come to the back door after dark. He would be arriving any minute, Mojo thought; the young man was never late.

He wasn't pleased at having to leave on such short notice or at having to distance himself from Josephine St. Claire. She had been a loyal worker and a generous lover. He would miss her. But, he told himself, he couldn't allow his personal feelings to interfere with the greater cause. He had accumulated over $12 million in diamonds and another million or so in cash, most of which was stashed in offshore accounts. It was enough to begin constructing the compound in St. Croix and take one more step toward his dream. He leaned back against the brick wall and patted the attaché case.

The familiar patterned knock on the door interrupted his thoughts.

"Shawayne?" Mojo shouted.

"Y-yes, Mojo . . . it's me."

Mojo stood, walked over to the heavy door, and began unlocking it. When he opened the second bolt, the door was pushed hard against him, and, as he stumbled backward, Shawayne was flung inside onto the dirt floor. Two men rushed into the room and slammed the door after them. Mojo caught only a fleeting glance of the two hulking figures before one shoved him down onto his stomach, clamped a heavy foot on his spine, and shouted, "Don't move and don't turn around."

Beside him, Mojo heard Shawayne pleading for forgiveness. "I'm sorry, Mojo! I didn't see them . . . they said they were gonna kill me if I didn't do it!"

"Shut the fuck up!" one of the men shouted.

A moment later, Mojo heard the pop of a silenced automatic weapon, and Shawayne collapsed beside him. Mojo reached for his revolver and struggled to turn over, but with his face pressed into the dirt and the weight of a foot on his back he couldn't move fast enough. The last thing he saw was a gloved hand reaching down to pick up the attaché case before the bullet crashed into the back of his skull. The men calmly left the room, leaving the door ajar, and walked through the adjacent abandoned building. The junkie who crouched amidst the building's debris and crumbling walls hardly noticed the two men, but his eyes lit up when he saw the partially opened door and swinging light in the building from which they had departed.

Kim Carlyle had arrived at her apartment around 8 P.M. and immediately called Lt. Jackson to let him know that she was safe. She was still shaken by the New Orleans events, so the presence of the uniformed officer outside her apartment was reassuring. Upstairs, she showered and bundled herself in a cotton gown before settling on the couch with a glass of French table wine. A Miles Davis-John Coltrane CD played on the stereo. She went over everything that had happened the day before, trying to find a pattern and integrate that information with what she had known before she went to New Orleans.

The more she scrutinized the facts available to her, the more confusing the puzzle became. There was no doubt now that the murders were the consequence of the diamond scheme. Something had gone wrong, Josephine said to herself. But what had it been and who was behind the murders? Mojo definitely had something to do with it, but he wasn't behind the wheel of the Mazda. Still, his stealing diamonds from a mobster was apparently the motive for Josephine's death and his disappearance. And if the Dutch hood, Kees, was also stealing, well, that might have led to his death. It seemed that the mob was very much involved in the killings, but aside from Kees and the mysterious Frank Napolini whom Josephine had mentioned, she had no information about organized crime. She hoped Lt. Jackson had discovered something.

And although she still couldn't bring herself to believe it, both Ruff Daddy and Klaus Svrenson could also easily be involved. In fact, after the call from Klaus, she was almost convinced that it was more of a threat than a warning. Was he trying to scare her off? Still, there were just too many holes, too many missing pieces of the puzzle.

At eleven o'clock when she turned on the TV news, several of those pieces suddenly surfaced. The lead story was a breaking news report in

Harlem. Clarence "Mojo" Johnson and a member of his religious sect, known only as Shawayne, had been found dead in the back room of the Old World Music Shop. A crack addict had discovered the bodies and informed police officers who were staked out in front of the premises. It was "apparently a gangland slaying," the reporter said as he stood outside the sealed-off murder scene. Another member of the sect, who had been called to identify the victims, indicated that Mr. Johnson and his chief assistant, Martin Latrell, had often argued during the past few weeks. Police officials said that Latrell was a former associate of Harlem drug and gambling kingpin Shabazz Pearson. Both were being sought for questioning. Pictures of Pearson and Latrell were flashed on the screen.

When Kim saw the photo of Latrell, she nearly dropped the ornate wine goblet that she held. She had seen him before, and it took only a minute for her to realize where. It was the same man that she had briefly glimpsed at Cheeno's Malibu party—the man who had turned and slipped away when she approached the African, Mawuli, and the two British businessmen. Kim was deep in thought, trying to figure out the connection, when the phone rang. It was Lt. Jackson, calling from his car.

"Have you heard what happened to Mojo?" he asked.

"Yes, yes . . . I just saw a report on TV."

"Well, that's not all. I—"

"Wait a minute Maurice! I know this Latrell. I saw him at the L.A. party, just before Cheeno was found dead. I recognized the photo."

"Latrell was in L.A. when Cheeno was killed?"

"Yes, and he was with two Englishmen and an African who said he was from Liberia. There has to be a connection, Maurice."

"Yeah, and there's something else. We got a report from authorities in Sierra Leone. Kwabena was murdered late Friday night in Freetown and, earlier the same day, Frank Napolini was killed in Ohio. It looks like someone is clearing the deck."

"Kwabena and Napolini? Then who's doing this, Maurice—who is behind it?"

"Look, Kim, it could be anyone—Svrenson, Pearson, Latrell, Ruff Daddy, who knows? The thing is, you're not safe. Whoever's behind it knows that you know too much. I'm putting another man outside your apartment right now. Don't leave without informing me. I want to know all you know about the people Latrell spoke to in L.A., but I can't talk with you now. I can't leave the murder scene. Latrell's our main suspect right now. He may not be the mastermind, but he's definitely involved with these killings. He knows something, and we need to know what."

"Okay, I'll talk to you tomorrow. But, tell me, what's your gut feeling about this? Who do you think is behind it?"

"I really don't know. But I'd put my money on Klaus or Ruff Daddy or both. We're still looking for them. And I wouldn't be surprised if one of them is working with Latrell or Shabazz Pearson. Diamonds are worth a lot more than policy slips or even crack cocaine. I think it's a take-over, a kind of coup, directed by someone who was already involved in the scheme and aided by someone with enough clout to back them up."

"Yeah, well, maybe you're right," Kim said resignedly. "I'll call you tomorrow."

Kim hung up the phone, turned off the lights and the television set, and checked that the door was securely locked before climbing the steps toward her bedroom for what she knew would be a night of fitful sleep.

FOURTEEN

New York—Sunday, August 5

Kim was awakened at 9:30 A.M. by the insistent ringing of her doorbell. She hadn't slept well, and her head still ached from the blow she had received in New Orleans. At the door, she peered through glazed eyes at a UPS deliveryman and the uniformed officer who stood beside him. "It's all right," the officer said when he noticed that the eyelet in the door had been opened. Kim unlocked the door, pulling her nightgown tightly around her shoulders.

The deliveryman offered an envelope. When Kim hesitated, the officer nodded his head and said, "It's okay, we checked the route from England. Everything seems in order."

England, Kim thought as she took the package and signed the receipt. "No bombs, then," she said, half smiling.

The officer shook his head no, and the visibly shaken deliveryman backed away from the door and hurried back to his truck. Kim thanked the policeman before shutting the door and going to her desk. The package had come from Sheffield, England, and had been sent by a Professor Winfred J. Blair. The location of origin and, of course, the name Blair immediately intrigued her. Expectantly, she tore open the envelope.

It contained a floppy disk and a handwritten note, which Kim quickly read.

Kim Carlyle:

I don't know you but I've discovered that my daughter called you just before her death. Apparently she trusted you. That's why I've sent the disk which accompanies this note. As you might expect, I'm deeply concerned with having those responsible for Mariana's death brought to justice. I'm not certain that the authorities here are aware of the breadth and scope of this situation. Since Mariana had begun a dialogue with you and you have been touched directly by these killings, I thought the information on the disk would be of particular interest to you. I was allowed into Mariana's apartment four days after her murder, when the authorities had finished searching the premises. My daughter always confided in me, so I knew where her notes were hidden. Although her computer had been confiscated, no one had found the notes that I've sent to you. They will, no doubt, retrieve the information from the computer in due time; and I'm sending another copy of the disk to Scotland Yard. I hope that this information will help in the search for those responsible for my daughter's murder. Please, keep me advised.

Sincerely,

Winfred J. Blair

After reading the note, Kim rushed to her computer and inserted the disk. The first entry was dated January 19, 2001. It noted Mariana's initial introduction to Kees Van derVall in Amsterdam and described her curiosity about his connection to Ruff Daddy. Kim quickly scrolled down, scanning the single-spaced pages on the screen. The last entry was dated July 30, the day Mariana died. Kim read carefully, hoping to discover a clue that might point to the reporter's killer. But there was no smoking gun, no decisive bit of information that clearly pointed to a person or a group of persons who may have been responsible for the killings, or even to a motive. Disappointed, Kim rose and went to the kitchen to put on a pot of coffee. When she returned to the desk, she printed the file then settled on the couch with the pages and a cup of strong black coffee. She reread the notes, underlining everything that seemed pertinent.

An hour and a half later, she rose and poured another cup of coffee. Returning to the couch, she hunched over the pages laid out on the coffee table, poring over the sixteen underlined entries.

> **FEB. 15** - Kees V. in London for two days, aside from hotel and drinks with Ruff Daddy, only stops are at De Beers Central Selling Office and a Mayfair flat, unable to determine who he saw.

> **MARCH 30** - Informants say police investigating Kees V.'s possible connection to heroin sales and gun smuggling—supplying arms to Sierra Leone Revolutionary United Front.

> **APRIL 5** - Amsterdam-K.V. & Petris N. meet young American at Grand Cafe, heated discussion. American registered as Riccardo Napolini at Swissotel Ascot. . . . Petris drives R. Napolini back to airport.

> **APRIL 6** - Klaus S. & Tiffany J. arrive in Amsterdam. Klaus meets Kees V. at De L'Europe Hotel night of Tiffany concert.

> **APRIL 7** - Tiffany leaves for Paris—loud argument with Klaus at airport. Kees accompanies Klaus to Antwerp. (activity unknown)

APRIL 8 - Ruff Daddy arrives, meets Klaus at De L'Europe. Both go to airport, take flight to Paris.

MAY 3 - Informant: Kees V. meets swarthy American at airport. Visitor stays in his apartment and rents car under the name Brian Woods????

MAY 14 - Confirmed, Brian Woods, low-level hood who worked at KCS Collection Agency in Los Angeles before moving to Las Vegas. KCS a subsidiary of a K. Svrenson parent company.

MAY 26 - Kees V. & Petris N. invite members of rap groups Watts Up and Kool Aid to a suite at the Renaissance Hotel on Dam Square after their concert. Entire group celebrates at 'Koepelkerk,' the landmark 17th-century reception hall across the street.

JUNE 6 - Kees V. and Ruff visit Lester B. at Paris apartment, then accompany him to funeral of Luther Olson, expatriate U.S blues singer who died of heart attack on stage??? Rendezvous at The Emerald Isle.

JUNE 19 - Introduced Brixton to Ruff, reluctantly!!!

JULY 9 - Kees and unidentified English business type visit T. Jones backstage after concert at The Palladium. They are followed by Asian woman and companion (appears to be Latino) when they leave.

JULY 10 - Petris N. leaves London on flight to Antwerp. Informant confirms that P.N. meets Kees V., they are seen in and around diamond district during next two days.

JULY 13 - Suspicious Asian woman spotted in Amsterdam, appears to be following Kees V. (informant) Who is she?

JULY 24 - Petris N. at De Beers, spends two hours inside. (contact unknown)

JULY 30 - Confirmed, R. Napolini nephew of Frank Napolini, Ohio mob underboss.

After an hour, Kim was certain that her suspicions about the deaths of the performers were correct. Somehow they had been involved in a scheme with Kees Van derVall and Klaus to smuggle diamonds into the country. Kwabena must have been the inside man in Africa. She also concluded that Cheeno had been involved, which would explain his high living even before he broke out as a popular recording artist. Clearly they had been shipping the gems back to the States in coffins, she'd derived that much from the encounter with Mojo in New Orleans. But the artists must also have been used in some other way. How?

What had gone wrong? Why were they killed?

After scrutinizing the notes again, she went to her computer and began checking foreign and domestic newspapers for information on Kees's Dutch associate and Frank and Riccardo Napolini. Without a last name, however, she was unable to find any references that matched Mariana Blair's scant description of Petris N. But a quick search of Las Vegas and Ohio newspapers revealed that Brian Woods had been murdered recently and that Frank Napolini's nephew, Riccardo, was among the chief suspects in his uncle's death. Neither story mentioned anything about diamonds; both incidents were considered mob hits. There were no named suspects in the Vegas murders, although police said that the killer knew the victims. Casino security guards were being questioned, but none had provided any useful information. In Ohio, authorities attributed Riccardo's possible involvement in his uncle's death to either his lingering anger over

Frank Napolini's complicity in the death of Johnnie Napolini, Riccardo's father, or an internal struggle for control over the Ohio mob.

Kim went back to the couch and, for the next four hours, continued poring over her own notes as well as Mariana's, trying to integrate all the information she had accumulated.

It was midafternoon when she called Lt. Jackson at the station. She told him about the arrival of the disk from Mariana Blair's father. Yes, she would immediately fax a copy, she assured him, before hurriedly describing its contents. She informed him of Mariana's findings about the previously unknown Dutchman Petris N. and the American Brian Woods. Woods, she told him, had been killed a day after Mariana was murdered in London. Then she pointed out that, according to Mariana, it was Riccardo Napolini, not Frank, who had been actively involved with Kees Van derVall and his associates in Amsterdam. Riccardo was also acquainted with the Dutchman Petris N.

Lt. Jackson listened in near silence. Throughout her rapid-fire recital, an occasional "Yeah" or acknowledging grunt was all Kim heard from his end of the line. She ignored the lukewarm response and continued.

"And I think you're right, Maurice, Klaus is probably behind the whole thing. I don't know how, but I'm sure he was using Tiffany, forcing her to help him smuggle gems into the country. She would never have been a part of this unless someone was making her do it. She was on her way back to the top—she wouldn't have risked ruining her career. And Klaus is the connection between this Woods character, a mob wanna-be who was also with Kees in Europe. Woods worked for Klaus in Los Angeles; he was recruited because of his mob ties. He's behind it, Maurice, the gem scheme and the murders."

"Kim, hold on a minute. There's something I need to tell—"

"No, listen! I've done some research, it makes perfect sense. The scheme probably started to unravel when Klaus discovered that Kees was not only skimming from him but also dealing arms for conflict diamonds with the rebels in Sierra Leone. Mojo was also robbing him blind. And poor Tiffany must have told him she wanted out. They had been cool toward each other since she returned from the last European tour. All of them had to be killed. And if that's true, then when Tiffany died the other artists, at least the key players who were apparently bringing gems in, also had to be eliminated. They knew too much, and they were afraid. Anyone involved in the old operation was a target, including mob guys like Woods and Frank Napolini. I wouldn't be surprised if Riccardo wasn't next. Klaus would have been forced to shift his alliances, find someone who was powerful enough to take them on. I think Klaus, Shabazz Pearson, and Mawuli, the African from Liberia, are behind it. Latrell and the Asian woman that Blair spotted in Europe were probably their paid henchmen."

"It's a fascinating theory, Kim, and most likely some of it's true," Lt. Jackson said. "The only problem, and you wouldn't let me tell you before, is that Klaus is dead. He was found by a groundskeeper in one of his posh secret getaways, a luxury cottage in Boca Raton, early this morning. His throat had been slit."

"What?"

"Wait, there's more. We discovered a note from the Plaza Hotel stuffed into the back of a pair of trousers that was folded in a suitcase. We think it was written on the night of Tiffany's murder; that's the last time Klaus stayed at the hotel. It's a list of twelve people, including a congressman, and it appears that he may have contacted them all. There were some phone numbers scribbled on the page. We checked them out and all of them except Ruff Daddy and, possibly, someone called 'Sally' are dead. We have an APB out for Ruff Daddy. And we'll find him soon, unless of course he's telling the truth. If he's really innocent, he's a target—someone might get to him first. And I gotta admit, I don't even know where to start looking for this 'Sally.'"

"It could be just a code name—she might have been working for Klaus," Kim said. "If everyone else on that list was involved in the operation, then we can assume that she was also."

"Yeah, but how? And is she still alive?"

Kim was silent.

"Klaus may have had something to do with the killings, or maybe not," Lt. Jackson continued. "But there's no doubt that right now someone else has stepped in. It could be someone like Ruff Daddy, I don't know. The note suggests that you're probably right about the initial scheme. Klaus probably set it up, and Tiffany may well have been trying to pull out. If she was killed, and I think she was, it seems to be the only motive for her death. Afterward, Klaus may have been trying to warn the others. I don't think most of them realized how deadly serious the situation was. And, again, I agree with you. There are some heavyweights involved. You don't snuff out a U.S. congressman or take on the mob, particularly someone like Frank Napolini, unless you're crazy or have some serious backup. But we're back to square one. The only advantage is that with the evidence we have now, the OCCB and the Feds will be more than willing to help."

Kim inhaled deeply and shook her head with resignation. She was still shaken by the news of Klaus's death and the realization that, if anything, the puzzle had become even more complicated. "Look, Maurice, why don't we meet at Henry's. I'll bring everything I have with me. You bring the list that Klaus left. I think that if we put our heads together, we can figure this out. I'm up to my neck in it now. I won't feel safe until we discover who's behind it."

"How about an hour from now?"

"Fine! I'm on my way, just tell those officers outside my door to stay put, okay?"

Who Killed Tiffany Jones? Contest Official Rules

Contest not open to residents of Maryland, New Jersey, North Dakota, Tennessee, and Vermont.

1. ENTRY Contest begins August 20, 2002. All entries must be received by March 1, 2003, and comply with these Official Rules to be eligible. To enter, please print or type your complete name, address, and zip code along with your answers on 8½" x 11" paper to the following four questions in the same order given below:

1) List three distinct methods used to smuggle diamonds into America.
2) Who is Sally?
3) Name the people behind the entire series of killings and explain the overall or primary motive for the murders.
4) For each of the following thirteen victims—Tiffany Jones, Kees Van derVall, Brixton Hewitt, K. J. Hunter, Dave Hamlin, Renee Rothschild, Cheeno, Mariana Blair, Brian Woods, Frank Napolini, Ezekiel Kwabena, Josephine St. Claire, and Clarence Johnson—answer the following questions:
   A) Who was the killer or killers?
   B) How was the victim killed?
   C) Why was the victim killed? (This answer will in some instances repeat the answer to the second part of question #3.)

Answers must be limited to five (5) 8½" x 11" double-spaced pages; not being more than two pages for questions #1 through #3 and no more than three pages for question #4. Make sure your name and address are clearly printed at the top of each page of your entry. Affix proper postage and mail your entry to: *Who Killed Tiffany Jones?* Contest Entry, P.O. Box 4319, Manhasset, NY 11030-4319. Limit one (1) entry per person per household and one entry per envelope. Entries become the property of Amistad, an imprint of HarperCollins*Publishers*, and will not be returned or acknowledged. Copies of *Who Killed Tiffany Jones?* are available at no charge for reading at various public libraries.

2. LIMITATIONS This contest is open to legal residents of the United States, excluding residents of Maryland, North Dakota, New Jersey, Tennessee, and Vermont, twenty-one years of age or older. Employees and the immediate families of HarperCollins*Publishers* Inc., their affiliates, parent companies, subsidiaries, Bill Adler Books, Marden-Kane, Inc., and the authors and their families, or any company involved in the development of this promotion are not eligible. Contest is void in the following five states and residents of these states are ineligible to participate: Maryland, New Jersey, North Dakota, Tennessee, and Vermont and wherever else prohibited by law. All entries must be the original work of the entrant only, created solely for the purpose of entering this contest. All federal, state, and local laws and regulations apply. Releasees (as defined below) are not responsible for printing errors or entries that are incomplete, lost, late, illegible, damaged, misdirected, or with postage due and such entries will be disqualified.

3. JUDGING The correct answers to the questions listed above in Paragraph 1 are based on clues found in the book, *Who Killed Tiffany Jones?* Only entries with complete answers to all parts of all four questions will be eligible for the prize. Answers will be judged by a panel of qualified judges based on correctness (60%), creativity (20%), clarity of expression (15%), and neatness (5%). In case of a tie: successive additional judges will grade such tied entries by the criteria listed above until the tie is broken. No alterations or forgeries will be accepted. Potential winner will be determined on or about March 22, 2003, by the judges, under the supervision of Marden-Kane, Inc., an independent judging organization whose decisions are final and binding. Such potential winner will be notified by mail.

PRIZE Grand Prize (1) $10,000. Taxes are the sole responsibility of the prizewinner. Potential winner will be notified by mail and will be required to complete and return a notarized affidavit of eligibility and liability/publicity release within 14 days of issuance or such potential winner will be disqualified. If prize or prize notification is returned as undeliverable, if potential winner does not return his/her affidavit of eligibility and liability/publicity release in a timely manner, or if potential winner cannot accept prize for any reason, the prize will be forfeited. The first runner-up in the judging will then be declared as the alternate winner, subject to compliance with these Official Rules. Winner grants permission for Sponsor and its designees to publicize such winner's name and/or photograph/likeness for advertising purposes without additional compensation except where prohibited by law. The prize is not transferable and no substitutions will be allowed. Winner agrees that HarperCollins*Publishers*, Bill Adler Books, Marden-Kane, Inc., their respective parent companies, subsidiaries, affiliates, advertising and promotions agencies, and all of their officers, directors, employees, shareholders, and agents (collectively, "Releasees") shall not be liable for injury, claim, loss, or damage of any kind resulting from participation in this promotion or from the acceptance or use of the prize awarded.

Odds of winning are dependent upon the nature and quality of the eligible entries received. No correspondence regarding entries will be entered into with non-winning entrants. Sponsor and its designees shall have the absolute, irrevocable right to use, assign, exploit, edit, modify, and publish the content of and elements embodied in any entry (and the entry itself) in perpetuity in any and all media (whether now existing or hereafter devised) and in any manner, for trade, advertising, promotional, or other use, or to dispose of any entry however they see fit, without further compensation or approval of entrants or any third parties.

5. WHO WON? and CORRECT ANSWERS For the name of the winner and for the correct answer to the questions listed above in Paragraph 1, available after April 1, 2003, send a stamped, self-addressed envelope no later than March 1, 2003, to *Who Killed Tiffany Jones?* Winner and Correct Answers, P.O. Box 4319, Manhasset, NY 11030-4319.

6. OFFICAL RULES For a copy of the Official Rules, send a stamped, self-addressed envelope no later than March 1, 2003, to *Who Killed Tiffany Jones?* Contest Official Rules, P.O. Box 4319, Manhasset, NY 11030-4319. Requests must be received by February 1, 2003.

Sponsor: HarperCollins*Publishers* Inc., 10 E. 53rd Street, NY, NY 10022
Administrator: Marden-Kane, Inc., 36 Maple Place, Manhasset, NY 11030

CREATORS

Bill Adler, author of more than 100 books, is a literary agent who represents such clients as Dan Rather, Larry King, and Mike Wallace, among others.

Mel Watkins, a former *New York Times Book Review* editor, is the author of *African American Humor: The Best Black Comedy from Slavery to the Present, On the Real Side : A History of African American Comedy,* and *Dancing with Strangers,* a memoir.

Both Adler and Watkins live in New York City.